RUN FOR THE MONEY

Frank Bryant cared little about money, but he cared greatly about righting any wrong he considered to have been done to him — like the slaughter of his partner, young Walt Summers. The fact that Frank almost died as well gave him extra incentive to square things with rancher Brad McLane. Then he tangled with McLane's wife, Angela, and he learned of McLane's real weakness. So Bryant went to work, aided by outlaws and the mysterious leader of a religious sect. But would he gain his revenge — and live to tell the tale?

CLAYTON NASH

RUN FOR THE MONEY

Complete and Unabridged

LINFORD
Leicester

First published in Great Britain in 2003 by
Robert Hale Limited
London

First Linford Edition
published 2005
by arrangement with
Robert Hale Limited
London

British Library CIP Data

Nash, Clayton
  Run for the money.—Large print ed.—
Linford western library
  1. Western stories
  2. Large type books
  I. Title
  823.9'14 [F]

ISBN 1–84395–766–3

Published by
F. A. Thorpe (Publishing)
Anstey, Leicestershire

Set by Words & Graphics Ltd.
Anstey, Leicestershire
Printed and bound in Great Britain by
T. J. International Ltd., Padstow, Cornwall

This book is printed on acid-free paper

For Michael James 'Everything',
Spiderman, Batman, Karate Kid
and Bob the Builder —
All rolled into one!

1

The Right Thing

They decided it would be best to do the right thing, seeing as how Bradford McLane was the man involved.

McLane was the big noise in this neck of the woods, owned more than half of Butte County, so much, in fact, there was talk about changing the name to *McLane County*. Whichever way you looked at it, he was rich and powerful and had the right ears in the state senate.

But there was something a little strange. It was whispered that for all that, McLane would never be elected governor. A small whiff of something in his past, corruption or graft or buying votes for the senator he wanted elected, nothing specific — still, the fact remained, he *could* have been governor on one or two occasions, but never pulled it off, and no one ever explained why.

Well, thought Walt Summers, what the hell? Most rich men in the West rode outside the law or used their power and money for their own ends, so if McLane had managed to get away with it so far, good luck to him.

There were some B Bar M cows mixed in with the mavericks he and his pardner, Frank Bryant, had rounded up in the Trinity Breaks. Walt wanted to keep them and try to sell them later, no questions asked. Frank wouldn't hear of it.

'Just as easy to do the right thing as not, Walt.'

'But we can use the money to develop our land!'

'We'll use our muscles instead.'

Walt let it go, but he had wondered before about this queer trait in his pardner: Bryant professed indifference to money. Sure, he'd work his butt off to earn some if he figured he needed it, but he insisted a man could get by without much money, live by his own skills and honour. One day he must ask Frank just what his aversion to money was. He'd once said, 'If you want to be rich, kid, don't stick with me.'

But Walt had done more than stick by Frank, he had even saved his life once . . . so, in the end, they decided to cut out the branded steers and take them back to McLane.

No sense in clashing horns unnecessarily, especially when they planned on being McLane's neighbours, Frank allowed.

They didn't know how McLane felt about that, but they soon found out when they drove the fifteen prime steers across Red Deer Creek and headed in towards the scattered tents and chuck wagon of the B Bar M camp.

Before they had travelled 200 yards from the creek, a bunch of riders came out of the brush and surrounded them. Both Bryant and Summers recognized McLane's ramrod, Fletch Kirby, as the man rode forward, a rifle across his thighs. Summers flung Bryant an uneasy look.

'Got his thumb on the hammer, Frank.'

'Just cautious. Hasn't recognized us yet.'

'The hell he hasn't!' Summers moved uncomfortably in his saddle, but was careful to keep his hands well in view, folded on the saddlehorn. 'It's only three weeks since he braced us in that saloon.'

'He was half-drunk.' Walt didn't know why Frank was making excuses for the solidly built, hard-faced Kirby. Maybe it was just a strong desire to keep things friendly: he wasn't a man who hunted trouble. There had been enough of that in his life over the past few years to last him clear into old age. At the same time, he wouldn't be wronged, either.

Now, he lifted a hand in a half-salute, smiling faintly. 'Howdy, Fletch. Looks like your boys've been busy.' He nodded towards the big temporary holding pens just this side of the scattered tents. They were crammed with rounded-up cattle. 'Lotta cows there.'

'I'm more interested in the bunch you're hazin',' Kirby said, in his deep-chested voice. He was a man in his mid-thirties, his hard-knuckled hands now lifting the rifle casually. Behind him, his three men took the cue and lifted their own guns. No hammers were cocked yet, but all the guns were pointing casually in the direction of Bryant and Summers. 'See our brand on that bunch you got there.'

'Yeah. Picked 'em up with some mavericks. Was bringin' 'em down to return 'em to you.'

Kirby smiled crookedly and his thin lips curled as he spoke out of the side of his mouth without taking his granite-like eyes off the riders. 'Boys — you hear that? We got us a couple of *honest* sod-busters here! I swear I never figured

I'd live to see the day. Returnin' our steers to us!'

Guffaws from the B Bar M riders, but no real mirth in the sound.

'Mr McLane'll be happy to know that, Fletch!' opined a tow-headed rider in torn shirt and battered brush chaps.

Kirby nodded gently, still staring hard and soberly at Bryant. 'Why don't you ride up and tell the boss about it, Steve? He might even want to meet these sod-busters, them bein' such . . . oddities.'

As Steve rode away, Bryant said a little tightly, 'We're homesteaders, not sod-busters.'

'That a fact? Din' know there was any difference. They both stink the same far as I'm concerned.'

Frank Bryant felt the coldness twist his guts into a pretzel. Summers cleared his throat awkwardly and his mount moved a little. The guns lifted, hammers cocking now.

'Judas, Frank!' breathed Summers, those big baby-blue eyes widening. He was several years younger than Bryant, still in his early twenties, face kind of gaunt and with a hangdog look that had almost every woman he met, regardless of her age, wanting to mother him.

Bryant was pushing hard at thirty-five, more experienced, with long years of hardship and self-sufficiency riding his broad shoulders. He was whip-lean, had a longish, square-jawed face and the wildest grey eyes this side of the Rio. They could be soft and warm or as cold as a pair of twin bullets about to enter a gun barrel.

His face showed nothing as he flicked those eyes now to Fletch Kirby. 'Why're you pushin' this, Fletch? You can see we were on our way down to B Bar M.'

Kirby shook his shaggy head. His eyes were green and cold as rim-ice on a winter's morn, his lantern jaw thrusting aggressively. 'Know nothin' of the such-which. You knew this camp was here?'

Bryant hesitated, then shook his head. 'No — saw it comin' down from the hills. We'd figured to head in to the main ranch originally.'

'Uh-huh. Seen us, so figured you better change your mind about keepin' them cows and try to talk us round.'

'You're just spoilin' for a fight, ain't you?'

Kirby smiled. 'With you? It wouldn't be any kind of a fight. Two hits: one when I hit you, other when you hit the ground.'

Bryant smiled thinly. 'You're not that good.'

Kirby stared back coldly for a long minute and without turning his head asked, 'Boss comin' yet, Pink?'

'Not yet, Fletch,' answered one of the B Bar M cowboys.

'Cover 'em.' Kirby started to dismount, saying to Bryant and Summers, 'Shuck your gunbelts. Now!'

They hesitated, Summers plainly going to take his lead from Bryant, but the latter nodded faintly and they unbuckled their belts and let them fall to the ground.

'C'mon on down, sod-buster,' Kirby said, striding forward swiftly and reaching up for Bryant.

But he took a boot in the face which sent him staggering and flailing wildly for balance half-way across the clearing. Startled, Fletch Kirby went down on one knee.

By the time he was thrusting to his feet. Bryant was upon him, closing fast, swinging both fists low, at his own hip-level. They took the rising foreman in the face and Kirby felt flesh split and lips mash back against his teeth. He spat some blood as he came roaring up, fists hammering as if driven by a cyclone.

Bryant staggered and stumbled, pushing one hand against the ground to keep from going down all the way. A boot lifted into his chest as he was stooped over and he sagged sideways, still not falling down. But a knee to the side of the head stretched him out and he blinked up through red mist as he saw a worn boot-heel driving down for his face.

He twisted violently aside, one ear

ripping, and then he was up, baring his teeth as he swivelled at the waist and interlocked his fingers, making both hands into a kind of clubbed hammer. Then he swung them as if holding an axe. He brought them down and around as Kirby closed in fast, powerful legs thrusting, big body moving like a charging buffalo . . . straight into those deadly locked hands.

The calloused edges of Bryant's hands met the other man's face, and the blood gushed as Kirby's nose broke and gristle and cartilage were driven back almost to the same plane as his high cheekbones. He stopped dead, big body shuddering. The force of Kirby's impact with the locked fists rocked Bryant on his feet. He had to shuffle quickly to keep his balance.

Kirby fell against him, splashing him with his blood, eyes crossed, head tilted back, body loose and without power now as he collapsed. Bryant knew it had been a lucky blow, Kirby's speed adding to the devastating effect, and he saw the utter shock on the faces of the cowboys with the guns that were still covering him and Summers. He had heard of Fletch Kirby's brutal reputation before he had arrived in Butte County, and while he hadn't looked forward to tangling with the man, he had figured a knockdown-drag-out fight was about the only language someone like Kirby would savvy.

Now it seemed he had done the impossible: knocked out Fletch Kirby, who was now twitching as he lay on the ground, his blood soaking into the dirt.

When Bryant looked up, he was surprised to see Bradford McLane sitting astride a big buckskin with an almost white mane, a beautiful black-haired woman several years his junior beside him on a palomino. Steve, the cowhand who had been sent to fetch them, had dismounted and was kneeling beside the groaning Kirby. His dust-smeared face was astounded as he looked up at McLane.

'Judas, boss! This sonofabitch has

beat Fletch's nose flat into his face!'

The buckskin jumped forward and Steve yelled as the animal's chest smashed into him and flung him spinning and rolling to sit in the dirt almost at the feet of Summers's grulla. He blinked as McLane leaned from the saddle and slashed his quirt across his shoulders, ripping Steve's grimy shirt and drawing blood and alarmed cries from the man.

McLane's face was ugly with rage as he looked down at the cringing cowboy. 'You watch your mouth around Mrs McLane!' He swung the quirt in one final slash and it took Steve across the face, laying a welt on his left cheek. The man howled and winced, grabbing at the stinging mark.

'Apologize!' gritted McLane, and the woman walked her palomino forward a couple of steps.

'Brad — it's not necessary. He was just so shocked at seeing Fletch beaten . . . ' the woman protested.

McLane rounded on her, eyes narrowing. 'I'll decide what's necessary and what isn't!'

Steve, seeing how he could come out of this even worse than he had already, quickly snatched off his sweat-greasy hat and, with a little blood trickling down his face, looked up at the young woman and said hoarsely, 'I beg your pardon, ma'am. I — I din' mean to — to cuss like that in front of you.'

She started to smile, then thought better of it, no doubt realizing it would only make things worse for Steve, and so nodded graciously and soberly. 'Apology accepted, Steve.'

She left it at that and Steve, shaking, remounted, mopping at the blood with his bandanna. The other cowboys were still covering Summers and Bryant, and now McLane turned his attention to the latter as Fletch Kirby swayed groggily on his feet, holding his neckerchief over his mauled face.

'Who're you?'

'Frank Bryant, Mr McLane. We met

13

briefly in Masthead outside Garrison's General Store a few weeks back.'

'What're you doing with my cows?'

'Returnin' them. Me and my pard were roundin' up mavericks and these were amongst 'em. We cut 'em out and were bringin' 'em down to you when Kirby and his crew jumped us.'

McLane looked down at the bloody and dusty ramrod. The rancher was a solid man, although not that tall. His width and girth gave the impression of a powerful man. He had a roundish face, smooth-skinned, with a small, straight nose, a wide, full-lipped mouth that had a pouty look to it, and eyes that could scratch a diamond, almost colourless — *spit*-coloured, Bryant thought, but kept the description to himself.

Those eyes flicked now to Kirby. 'Well, Fletch?'

'They were aimin' to drive the cows up into the butte country, where they could sell 'em cheap to those hard-rock ranchers in there. Saw our round-up camp comin' down the high trail and turned yaller, decided they might's well bring 'em in and save themselves some trouble, is my guess.'

His speech was slurred, throaty.

'You're lyin',' Bryant said easily, but Kirby didn't rise to the bait. He knew he had his boss's ear. The man actually gave Bryant a twisted smile.

'Just how do you know what Mr Bryant had in mind, Fletch?' asked the woman.

They all looked at her quickly and she seemed slightly startled, Bryant thought, as she became the centre of attention. She stirred, gave back a somewhat defiant stare.

'I mean — can you read people's minds?'

McLane was watching her soberly, eyes narrowed, cold.

Fletch Kirby shrugged. 'I know sod-busters, ma'am. Not a single one of 'em worth the powder it'd take to blow 'em away.'

The girl bristled. 'Now that's going too far!'

'Angela!' McLane's voice cut through anything more the girl might have had to say. She snapped her head up and around at the lashing sound of her name, swallowed when she looked into the rancher's face. 'Go back to the house.'

'There's no need for that, Brad.' There was a tremor in her voice, but she kept her defiant look as she started to lift her reins. 'I'll just ride along the river as we set out to do in the first place.'

'You'll go back to the house! *Now!*'

She flinched at the whipcrack of the word at the same time as his quirt thongs slapped viciously against his corduroy riding britches, just above his polished halfboots. His eyes were burning now like twin coals, ready to blaze into the flames of full anger.

She flushed and her eyes briefly rested on Bryant's face as she wheeled the palomino, raked with the spurs and sent the animal splashing into the creek, making for the trail that led back to B Bar M ranch headquarters.

Impassively, McLane watched her go, and his eyes gradually lost their murderous look and reverted to their normal cold stare as he set them on Bryant.

'I hear you're aiming to homestead that quarter-section north of my ridge line.'

'That's the idea.'

McLane shook his head. 'Not any more. I need that land for graze.'

Bryant stiffened. 'You're kiddin'! With the thousands of acres you've already got . . . ?'

'I — need — that — land,' he said slowly.

'You're too late. Walt and I filed on it two days before we started roundin' up mavericks.'

McLane merely smiled crookedly. 'I wouldn't bet that file found its way to the Lands Department, Bryant.'

'Why, you greedy sonofa — ' Bryant started forward, but he had been giving all of his attention to McLane when he should have watched Kirby.

The ramrod clubbed him to his knees with the butt of his sixgun, planted a boot between his shoulders and shoved so that Bryant fell on his face in the dirt at McLane's feet.

The rancher didn't even bother looking at him, spoke to his ramrod. 'We still hang rustlers on the spot in this state, Fletch. But, then again, Bryant's left his mark on you. You want to handle it?'

Kirby lowered his blood-soaked kerchief and his eyes glittered. 'You mean it, boss?'

'Any way you like.'

McLane mounted the buckskin, looking at the three cowhands, settling his gaze on the ramrod.

'Any way you like, Fletch,' he repeated, wheeled the mount and spurred away across the creek, following the trail taken by his wife.

Despite the pain it must have cost him, Kirby grinned coldly as he looked at the two homesteaders.

'Well, boys, now what're we gonna do with these fellers? I ain't gonna hang 'em. That's too good for 'em. Let's give the matter a little thought, huh?'

Walt Summers swallowed and looked towards Frank Bryant, whose face was deadpan.

But those wild grey eyes didn't flicker as they bored into Fletch Kirby.

There was a silent promise of death in them for the big ramrod.

2

Revenge

Fletch and his men took the homesteaders way back into the Breaks, beyond the boundaries of the B Bar M, into the isolated regions where only wild animals — both four-legged and two — roamed.

By the time they got there, Bryant and Summers were conscious, but it was no great shakes being that way. They were roped to their mounts, and as soon as Fletch Kirby saw that they had come round, he rode in close and lashed both of them with his quirt, drawing blood from their already battered faces. They rocked in the saddles and the foreman grinned, although it was hard to be sure — his face was all puffy and bruised, streaked with dried blood, his nose a squashed pulp. He breathed through his mouth constantly, spitting gobbets of blood and mucus from time to time.

Swelling hid the mean look in his eyes, but it was there in his tone of voice.

'Won't be long now, Bryant! You and the kid are gonna see the error of your ways!'

'Leave the kid out of it, Kirby, it's me you want.'

Kirby gave a short laugh, and spat again. 'Hell, I've got you. Both of you. Might's well be hung for a sheep as a lamb, they say. Or, kill two birds with the one stone — which one you like best?'

'Leave him be,' Bryant said, a deadly edge to his voice, which was picked up by Steve and Pink. The cowhands glanced a trifle uneasily at each other.

There was something unnerving about the way Bryant spoke, even though he was in no position to be making threats.

Kirby slashed him again with the

quirt and rode on ahead, disappearing around a boulder-strewn bend. The others urged Bryant and Summers on, and they found Kirby waiting on a small rise, hands on the saddlehorn as he leaned his weight on it.

'Take a look, Bryant.' He gestured with a jerk of his head to somewhere beyond the rise.

Bryant's mount climbed the slope slowly, Summers looking apprehensively at his pard as he followed. He came up alongside Bryant and snapped his aching head around.

'The hell's he got in mind, Frank?' Walt Summers asked, puzzled.

Bryant said nothing, instinctively tried to work his hands free of the rope binding them to his saddlehorn, but all it did was make the rope rip more skin from his wrists.

Below was broken ground, covered in shards of rock and stretches of ancient pumice, spat out of the earth's bowels long ago in the dim shadows of time. It was a long, shallow slope that stretched away into a flat perspective covered in chaparral and sagebrush, lifting away towards distant grey walls of canyons that no one had explored in living memory.

Kirby forced his mount between the homesteaders. 'Now, you two've been bad boys, tryin' to rustle Mr McLane's cows. But he's been generous, din' string you up on the spot like he had every right to do — but that don't mean you're gonna get off. He gave you to me, see? An' it's up to me to decide your punishment.'

'Just decide for me, Kirby,' Bryant said in that quiet, deadly voice. 'I'll ask you one more time — will you let the kid go?'

'I'm stayin' with you, Frank!' Walt Summers said hoarsely, pale now, knowing they were both dead men.

'See? Kid wants to stay,' Kirby grinned. 'Never let it be said that Fletch Kirby was too mean an' ornery to grant a man's last wish.'

Bryant's chill gaze stopped Kirby as

he dragged down a breath to add more. 'You're a dead man, Kirby.'

The threat was delivered quietly, in a conversational tone, and maybe because of that it sent a cold tremor down Steve's spine and he licked his lips as he glanced at Pink and Carlos, the third cowhand, before flicking his eyes to the ramrod's shattered face.

But Kirby wasn't bothered by any threats. He sneered and back-handed Bryant, rocking the man in the saddle. For good measure, he dealt the same kind of blow to young Walt and Summers swayed, spitting a broken tooth and some blood.

'Now, what's gonna happen is this,' Kirby said, in almost the same conversational tone Bryant had used a few moments earlier. 'We're gonna take you boys down there to the edge of the brush — no, we might even drag you into the middle of the brush.' He flicked his bruised and swollen eyes from one man to the other. 'Then we're gonna turn you loose . . . '

He said no more, watching them expectantly. Bryant said nothing, his face blank, but Walt just had to ask, 'Turn us loose? You're lettin' us go?'

'I said we'd turn you loose — what you do after that is up to you. If you can find your way out, good luck to you, but there's a hell of a lot of brush in there, and it backs up on to that rock wall — and we'll be settin' down there at this edge just waitin' to see what happens . . .'

Walt frowned, not yet understanding, looking at Bryant. 'We gotta run the gauntlet of their guns, Frank?'

'Could come to that, Walt.' Bryant's voice was tight as he glared at the smirking Kirby.

'Then, we got a fightin' chance . . . ?'

Bryant stared back, hearing the guffaw from Fletch Kirby. Not even his men had figured it out, it seemed.

'Tell him, Bryant!' Kirby chuckled. 'Tell him how much of a chance you've got!'

Summers was looking really worried now. 'Frank?'

Still Bryant hesitated, and Kirby snapped some orders and Pink and Carlos dropped ropes over the bound men while Steve cut their bonds, freeing their hands from the saddle-horns. At another sign from Kirby, the ropes were pulled tight and yanked hard, spilling Bryant and Summers out of their saddles.

They crashed to the ground and Kirby yelled and fired two shots into the dirt beneath the mounts of Pink and Carlos. The horses reared and snorted, and with the prodding of their riders' spurs, lunged down the steep slope, dragging the homesteaders after them.

'Oh, God, Frank!' cried Summers, as dust choked him and his body twisted as he was dragged like a rolling log down the slope towards the waiting stones and pumice. 'We'll be cut to pieces!'

Bryant didn't — couldn't — answer,

but he knew being dragged at the end of a rope across those rocks would be only the beginning. Once they reached the brush, probably unconscious, certainly dazed and bruised and bleeding, they would be hauled into the centre of that huge spread of bushes — and abandoned.

Then, when his men had ridden out again, Fletch Kirby would set fire to the brush, with Bryant and Summers lying bleeding and barely conscious in its midst.

And with nowhere to go, except a high, unclimbable stone wall — or the waiting guns of Kirby and his men.

★   ★   ★

Angela McLane was still removing her riding gloves when she heard her husband's horse downstairs in the ranch yard. She walked to the window, not touching the lace curtains, watching as he dismounted by the corrals, snapped something to the Mexican kid who ran across from the barn, and then strode towards the porch and out of her sight.

She sighed: she knew by that heavy striding lurch and the way he slapped his quirt against his trousers that he was in a bad mood. There was a flutter in her breast and a lurch in her stomach, but she knew it was no use trying to run or hide — already he was clumping up the stairs, calling her name.

'In here,' she answered, quietly and reluctantly.

She turned to face him as he came in, slamming open the door. He stopped a few feet in front of her and watched her compose herself. Involuntarily, she stepped back a pace as he shook a thick finger under her nose.

'Don't you ever do that again!'

'What was it this time?' Angela flinched as, for a moment, she thought he was going to strike her with his quirt. But he held back.

'You took the side of that goddamn sod-buster! Tried to make Fletch look foolish! Sure as hell made me look that way. A man in my position, with no control over his wife? No respect from her, not enough decency to back her husband no matter what? How you think that looks? Eh?'

Her gaze faltered. She hadn't seen him as mad as this for a long, long time. And the memories of that time made her tremble so that she clasped her hands in front of her to prevent it showing. She fought to keep her voice steady.

'Fletch Kirby was claiming to know what that man Bryant was thinking! It wasn't fair.'

'Fletch had the good sense to back me, and that was his way of letting me know! Damn you, Angela! You're becoming more and more of a problem. An embarrassment!'

He strode across the room, glanced out the window, then tore the lace curtain as he wrenched it aside and leaned out, berating the Mexican roustabout for not allowing the horse to cool before leading it to the water trough. He swore savagely; it always amused Angela the way he would literally jump on any man who cussed or used off-colour words within her hearing, but made no attempt to temper his own profanity.

'Greasers! I don't know why I keep them on! Now, this is the last time I'm warning you, Angela: *keep your mouth shut* when I'm conducting my affairs.'

'If you want to be respected, Brad, you have to learn what's fair and what isn't.'

He blinked. This was the first time she had spoken to him like that. And she continued quickly, a slight tremor in her voice now.

'Those two homesteaders were obviously going to return your cattle, and you wrongly accused them of rustling. What's more, Brad, you *knew* it was wrong.' She shook her head. 'I can't — and won't — keep quiet under such circumstances! Two men's lives were dependent on your interpretation of things — and you chose the worst possible way to look at it, because you want the land that Bryant was planning to home-stead, or you *say* you do. You don't need that land at all! It's straight-out cussedness, and a cold-blooded disregard for human life. Dress it up any way you choose, but you're nothing but a greedy damn landgrabber!'

The last word was crammed back into her teeth by the open-handed blow that snapped her head back on her shoulders and sent her sprawling across the bed. She lay there, gasping, one hand to her stinging face, eyes blurred with tears. She felt his fingers twist painfully in her long, dark hair, and her head was wrenched back, stretching her throat. She smelled the last cigar he had smoked on his breath as he gritted words against her ear.

'Mind — your — own — goddamn — business!'

Then he thrust her face into the soft bedcovers, a knee jammed between her shoulders, smothering her, yanking her head back and forth as she choked and bucked in panic and her breath was cut off. He kept swearing at her, pushing hard on the back of her head, his face congested with rage, until, finally, he realized her struggles were growing weaker, and then he heaved her on to her back, flinging her to the floor.

She lay on her side, terrible croaking noises and harsh wheezing and gagging sounds coming from her throat as she fought for air. He towered above her, his face totally devoid of compassion. He nudged her spine with his boot.

'You heed me, woman! Stay out of my business! I can do what I like here, or anywhere else for that matter. And you'll go along with it, whether you like it or not. Now, you remember that, or it'll be the worse for you!'

He leaned over her, made sure her tear-filled eyes were focused on him and then shook her, delivering a final stinging blow to her swollen and blotchy face. 'Believe me!'

Then he whirled round and strode out, leaving the door swinging.

Angela began to sob as, at last, air was sucked into her burning lungs. She lay there, waiting to recover, fear making her nauseous.

From her position, she could see a dark-grey column of taffy-twist smoke rising far back over the peaks in the Trinity Breaks.

Forgetting her agony momentarily, she thought, My God, that's one mighty big brush-fire!

* * *

The flames were twenty feet high and climbing.

The heat blasted off the precipitous rock wall, driving back Fletch Kirby and his men. The battered ramrod swore, his eyes stinging, throat burning from the smoke. *Damnit*! He wanted to see Bryant and Summers burning!

They hadn't been in very good shape after the drag across the rocky approach to the clump of chaparral, clothes torn, flesh cut, bruised and bleeding. But there had been life in them a'plenty, and that was what Kirby wanted.

He wanted them to *know* they were burning alive, and that he had done it to them. Fingering his mashed nose gently, he smiled, ignoring the stretching of his mauled facial muscles. Yeah! He had gotten his own back on Bryant, and treating Summers the same way had only added to Frank Bryant's own suffering.

This had been a damn good idea — hell, it was *brilliant*! It showed his men — who would spread the word — that Fletch Kirby was definitely not a man to mess with (as if half the county didn't already know that!) — and at the same time he had the satisfaction of inflicting pain on the man who had disfigured him.

Now the fire was roaring completely out of control, sweeping through the brush like some sort of infernal incoming tide, devouring everything before it — including Bryant and his kid partner.

Well, he couldn't see it, and he sure as hell couldn't hear their screams over the thunderous sucking roar of the flames, but he knew what was happening, could picture it clearly, the smoke choking his victims, blinding them as they instinctively struggled in their semi-consciousness to crawl away from the fire, having no chance. Then the flames scorching the soles of their boots, popping the stitches; the stinking, smouldering leather dropping away to expose the tender flesh; the blistering, the searing . . . Then the clothes flaring on their bodies, their hair ablaze.

Fletch Kirby grinned widely, a little blood oozing from the stretched corners of his mouth, folded his hands on the saddlehorn, and sat back, his men huddled behind him, watching.

★ ★ ★

35

Kirby's imagination was very close to reality.

Frank Bryant's feet were agonizing as his boot soles fell away and the heat blistered his flesh. He bit back a cry and twisted aching fingers more tightly into the shirt of the unconscious Walt Summers. The kid had taken a heavy blow on the head when being dragged across those rocks, and he hadn't really come round since.

Summers had given a few moans and once opened his eyes after he and Frank had been dumped in the middle of the brush and Pink and Carlos had ridden back to the edge where Kirby and Steve waited. Then Kirby's men had set fire to the sage and chaparral as Bryant had predicted.

He was moving, painfully and with great effort, before he heard the first crackling of the flames taking hold. There was really nowhere to go, but the rocky wall afforded them their only chance. The other way was doubly dangerous, since they would be forced to run the gauntlet of both fire and guns.

Kirby had sent a man around each side, cutting off any chance of escape that way, too.

No, their only hope, slim though it was, lay in the direction of the wall. It might only postpone the inevitable, but that was preferable to lying there waiting for the flames to devour them.

Bryant was lucky insomuch as his hat was still somehow jammed on his head. Summers had lost his during the drag and bits of his hair were already alight. Frank paused to slap at it, feeling the heat against the palm of his hand, knowing it was useless. When the rest finally burst into flames, young Walt Summers screamed without showing any sign of consciousness returning. Desperately, almost totally blind in the swirling, stinging smoke, Bryant heaved his upper body across and used hands and forearms to beat at Summers's hair. He was only partially successful; felt heat on his trousers. His shoulders were already painfully sore as his shirt began to smoulder. Rolling over and over in an attempt to put out any flames that were taking hold on his clothing, he flung himself back to where he had left Summers, grabbed his shirt collar and tried to drag him behind, but found it easier to push and roll the man.

He had no idea where he was going and the flames were thundering in his ears, the tremendous noise disorienting him. He glanced up, thought he saw the loom of the rock wall but couldn't be sure. Not that it mattered; they weren't going to get out of this.

In fact, Summers was the lucky one: he was unconscious already. It wouldn't be long before Bryant was the same way. Breathing became harder and there was little air even with his face pushed against the ground. Dust and leaves made him sneeze repeatedly and each time he seemed to choke, had to fight down the ever-rising panic.

He was moving by instinct, not thinking now, way past that. Each heave of Summers's inert body cost him dearly. But he kept going — hell, what else was there to do? Leave the kid and try futilely to save himself?

Unthinkable! If he was going to die, then he was going to die doing what he could to help Walt Summers.

The kid would have done the same for him, he knew that. In fact, he had, not long ago — jumped into a flooded river when a cutbank gave way and Frank and his horse had tumbled into the raging rapids. And Frank Bryant couldn't swim . . .

Suddenly, he fell flat, clothes afire now, and he rolled wildly, throwing dirt over himself.

Then he realized he was sliding down a slope, short but steep. He was brought up hard against rock, tried to push up to get a better idea of where he was — and struck his head on more rock.

Even as he crawled back, groping for Summers so he could pull the youngster in with him, Bryant knew they had fallen into a hollow *beneath* the rock wall at its base — and therefore beyond the reach of the flames that were leaping in a solid line as they devoured the last of the brush in this area.

Exhausted, fighting the curtain of blackness that descended upon him like heavy wet canvas, he slid back, feeling Summers's body crash down on top of him.

3

Rimrock

Steve Macklin didn't want any part of this. He was sick just thinking about the part he had already played in burning those two homesteaders alive.

It didn't matter that Fletch Kirby had forced him to do it. *Forced?* Well, he had, sort of — just by being there and ordering him to come along and lend a hand. Steve knew he ought to have turned and ridden away, just kept on going, right away from B Bar M and its power-crazy owner. He had been about to pull his mount around and kick home the spurs, but as he was half-way turned, his gaze had locked with Kirby's. The foreman had lowered the blood-soaked kerchief from his mangled face, half-smiled at him and shaken his head — just barely, the slightest of movements. His right hand had strayed towards his gun butt, and Steve Macklin knew he would stop a bullet between shoulders if he tried to ride away.

So, scared white of Kirby, ashamed to admit it but knowing he was too weak not to, he had settled in and followed the ramrod's orders.

Now he was still following orders, riding the smoking ragged edge of the brush line, seeing only ashes and a few smouldering twigs, his horse rearing away in protest.

'Goddamit!' Kirby growled at his three men. 'Get in there and see if you can find what's left of the sonsofbitches. *Anything!* Melted belt buckles, charred bones! Just bring me proof that I can take back to Mr McLane.'

'We'll have to wait till nigh on sundown for the ground to cool after a fire like that, Fletch,' protested Pink. When Kirby back-handed the cowboy, Steve was glad he had held his tongue, although he had been about to say the very same words.

'Then we wait, goddamit,' Kirby roared, fighting his own skittish mount. 'We wait, but we go in before dark, whether it's cooled down or not! I want that proof!'

'No one could survive that, Fletch,' Steve ventured, and flinched at Kirby's chilling gaze, but Carlos spoke up and diverted the foreman's attention.

'Steve is right, Fletch. They're dead. We won't find nothin'.'

'Well, we're gonna try, you savvy?' Kirby raked all three with his gaze. 'We're — gonna — try!'

They all nodded glumly, wanting out of this, away from this spooky place.

Then suddenly Steve pointed along the top of the wall. 'Someone's watchin'!'

They all looked up, saw a movement, a shadow melting into other deeper shadows of the boulders and trees.

'Was that a rider?' Kirby sounded breathless, sliding his rifle out of leather, his face showing concern, enough to be visible beneath his injuries.

'Looked like it to me!' Steve breathed. 'But who the hell could be up there? There ain't no way up . . . '

'Not from this side, leastways,' allowed Pink quietly, and all eyes swung to him. 'I've heard tell for years that there's outlaws livin' in there. Smoke might've brought 'em.'

Kirby spat. 'Ah, all the old daisies've been seein' spooks in there. It's just injun talk. They claim that country's sacred. No one's ever found a way in to prove anythin', one way or t'other.'

Carlos crossed himself. 'To be sure, that was a man on a horse we see, Fletch.'

'So what if it was? He couldn't've seen anythin' from up there. Smoke would've blinded him. Far as he knows, we just come to see what was burnin'. Forget him. Have a smoke while we're waitin' for the ground to cool.'

They backed-up their mounts and were almost to a line of rocks when

44

guns crackled in a ragged volley from the rim of the high wall. Startled, they hunched over their mounts' necks as the lead spattered on the boulders behind, one ricocheting and bringing a surprised cry from Pink.

'Judas! That was no spook! I been hit!'

They saw the fresh, bright blood on the hand that he clasped against his side, and then another volley sent them racing for cover. One shot brought down Steve Macklin's mount and he hit hard, skidding through the dust, bringing up with a bang against the base of a large boulder. None of the others tried to help him, as, dazed, he got to his knees and started to crawl towards the shelter of the rocks. Dust spurted from the back of his shirt and he yelled as he was punched forward by the impact of the lead. His head slammed against the rock and he fell unconscious, bleeding.

By that time, Kirby, Pink and Carlos were answering the gunfire on the rim, but they had only phantoms to shoot at.

Smoke hung in a haze on the rim, but not steady enough to pinpoint any one spot. Then the guns barked from further along to the left — and another two opened up from the right, raking the boulders with fire. The cowmen flattened as ricochets swarmed about them and Kirby said, 'Hell with this! Let's get outa here!'

The others needed no second bidding and, keeping the boulders between themselves and the high rim, they jumped into their saddles and spurred away, leaving Steve's body where it lay.

A final volley from the rim hurried them on their way . . .

* * *

The sounds cut through the pain and delirium that had gripped Frank Bryant. He coughed rackingly, and when the sounds had died away in the dark hollow where he lay, Walt's inert form pinning his lower body, he heard the rattle of gunfire — no mistaking it. He had heard too much of it in his life to be wrong about this.

He moaned involuntarily, feeling like a half-cooked steak, a little flesh sloughing off one shoulder when he tried to move. Teeth gritted, he lifted his head slowly, ash and charred twigs falling from the curled brim of his scorched hat. Distant ricochets sounded like wasps angrily buzzing around a disturbed nest. Then he heard the clatter of fast-moving horses, still distant, and a harsh, more intense crash of gunfire. This seemed to come from fairly close by, but he had no real sense of direction.

Then all was silent except for the roaring in his ears and his own coughing and laboured breathing. He couldn't tell if Walt Summers was still alive or not. He tried holding a breath, but he wasn't taking in enough air to hold it for more than a few seconds. Far as he could tell, there were no signs of life in his badly-burned pard.

His own hands were blistered and he

thought he might have lost the little finger on his left hand. His vision was badly blurred and he blinked furiously, making tears come to flush some of the ash and grit from his eyes.

It didn't do a lot of good, but then he heard something above him and he looked up in time to see some kind of shapeless shadow move across the band of daylight.

And the sound that came after that could only have been the cocking of a gun hammer, as a hard voice said, 'You got five seconds to come outa there, then I start shootin' — an' friend, I don't like your chances of dodgin' my lead in that there place where you're hidin'. I'll give you the five, but no more. One, two, three . . . '

'Give 'em both a bullet. You'll be doin' 'em a favour.'

Logan flicked his eyes towards the big man who had spoken. He didn't answer for a short interval, even though a couple of the others backed the big man's suggestion. 'I think I know this one,' Logan said eventually, and nudged the prostrate form of Bryant, the man's clothes burned through in a dozen places. 'Not sure of his name, but I think I seen him in El Paso. Outdrew Drag Magee. Nailed him dead-centre, single shot, din' even wait to see if he'd killed him. But Drag was dead on his feet, and this *hombre* knew it, just holstered his gun and walked away before Drag even hit the ground.'

'How can you recognize anyone under all them burns and that dirt?' asked Ned Nudge, the big bearded man who wanted to put Bryant and Summers out of their misery.

'It's him; I'm almost sure. This other one don't look as if he'll pull through, though.' Logan levered a shell into his rifle and started to draw a bead on Walt's head when the man moaned and rolled his head to one side. Logan jumped. 'Judas!'

The others laughed: big joke. But Logan, a handsome man, his face stubbled and a little grimy from hard riding, lowered his gun hammer. 'We'll take 'em with us.' The men with him stirred and he looked hard at them. 'They were bein' hunted by Fletch Kirby and some of McLane's scum, weren't they? That gives 'em a plus in my book.'

'Gonna give us a lotta damn work for nothin',' growled Nudge, and a couple of the others agreed.

'But if this one's who I think he is, and he's got a hate on for McLane and Kirby — man, we got us an asset.'

'What about the other one? Looks no more'n a kid.'

'If they're pards, he'll know how to handle a gun, too. This one would see to that.'

'What about Steve Macklin?' asked another man, raw-boned, grubby, his clothes patched and mismatched. He was known as Curly. 'He's still alive.'

'Bring him,' Logan ordered. 'He can give us information about McLane.' They hesitated as he looked at them one at a time. 'Handle 'em gently till

Doc gets a look at 'em. Now move! That smoke could bring in a lot more folk we don't want to see.'

Mumbling and grumbling, the men moved to obey Logan, who stood looking down into the dark slash of the rock cleft under the high wall. Whoever these fellers were, they were mighty lucky to have fallen into it.

Otherwise, they wouldn't even be distinguishable from all that smouldering black ash that stretched for a mile back towards the canyon entrance.

Yeah, mighty lucky!

★　★　★

Three weeks after the big fire, Angela McLane rode into the town of Masthead and went to a small house in a side street. A man named Fly lived there, a watchmaker by trade who also dealt in jewellery. Looking through some old papers she kept in a box, cards and letters from friends and her family, Angela had come across a small watch on a short length of gold-coloured silk ribbon, with a real gold pin at the top. It was a watch that had been used by her mother when she had nursed wounded men under Miss Florence Nightingale during the Crimean War. It wasn't in working order, and so she decided, in a fit of nostalgia, to see if Mr Fly might think it worth restoring.

She smiled as she went through the gate and read the hand-painted sign tacked to one upright: *TIME 'FLIES' — but not here! Isaac Fly can control it. See him for all clock and watch repairs. Reasonable rates. Best workmanship.*

Mr Fly was a small, nimble man with a hunched back from stooping over the works of watches and clocks for more than thirty years. He told her the watch could be repaired, but that he would need to make some new parts for it.

'I would need the piece for perhaps three weeks. A month, if I can't match the parts and have to send for them back East. It will be quite expensive, Mrs McLane.'

'That's quite all right. I want it repaired, if it's at all possible.' A little ruefully, she added, 'Send the bill to my husband.'

Mr Fly smiled under his drooping moustache. 'Of course. A generous man.'

Angela smiled slightly. 'He — can be.'

'Most assuredly! You — er — liked the sapphire necklace?'

Her smile disappeared and she frowned slightly, feeling a stiffening within her. 'Sapphire . . . ?'

Mr Fly looked quite serious now. 'Oh, yes; I gave Mr McLane my assurance that they were genuine stones, quality-cut into the best arrangement of facets. You must have noticed how well they sparkled . . . ? I went to a great deal of trouble to obtain them.' Then suddenly he put a hand to his mouth, a small finger tapping his lips. 'My goodness me! I

— I trust I haven't been indiscreet and spoiled the surprise?'

'Oh, it was meant to be a surprise? For me?'

'Yes, for your birthday. Why, I believe that would be today's date. You haven't received the necklace yet?'

Angela forced a smile. 'Not yet — but I believe Brad said he's taking me to the Masthead Ritz for supper tonight. He'll probably give it to me then.'

Mr Fly smiled widely. 'Of course. I'm terribly sorry if I've spoiled anything . . .'

'Quite all right, Mr Fly, quite all right.'

'Well — happy birthday, Mrs McLane.'

She left quickly and took the long way home.

Her birthday had been a month ago and McLane had given her the palomino. And he'd said he had a 'business' supper to attend tonight with other members of the Butte County Cattlemen's Alliance . . .

★ ★ ★

Angela stayed in and read some Dickens that evening, and her husband did not return until almost daylight. He said the 'business' had dragged on and then the men had played poker into the small hours. He smelled of booze — and a rather nice perfume she knew was imported, because she had a small, dark-blue bottle of it herself on her dressing-table. It was called *Soir de Paris* — Brad had assured her she was the only woman in this part of the country who had any.

Late in the afternoon he went riding, ostensibly to check on the rounding-up of more mavericks. She followed at a distance, seeing almost immediately that he was not heading towards the area being worked by Fletch Kirby and his men.

He was making for the river trail, and she had no trouble following and staying out of sight because there was plenty of timber. About four o'clock he turned towards a secluded bend they had gone to on several occasions when they were courting.

Her heart beating fast, she rode a high trail up to a ridge of rimrock overlooking that bend, dismounted and took a pair of field-glasses from her hand-tooled saddle-bag.

The lenses soon picked up McLane's horse, tethered to a side wheel of a surrey amongst some bushes. She recognized that surrey — it belonged to Millicent Handel, owner of Masthead's largest dress-makers' store.

Her hands trembled, and she felt sick — and angry — as she watched them sitting on a tartan blanket, embracing passionately. Then the red-haired woman slowly reclined, and McLane followed, not breaking the kiss, one hand groping beneath Millicent's voluminous skirts.

Angela drew in a sharp breath: but that was not the part of Millicent Handel's anatomy she was interested in.

The dying sun's rays flashed brilliantly from a blue sapphire necklace standing out against the pale skin of the woman's throat.

4

Tribes of the sun

It was a settlement like no other that Bryant had seen.

He had been here three weeks now and still found it hard to come to terms with this place called Huntka-Wi, the God of the East, or, the Sun. The people called themselves Sun-Christians.

'We follow Christian teachings, but we worship the sun as the image of God, or, as we prefer to call Him, The Life-Giver.'

This was told to Bryant by Doc Hubbard, leader of the religious group. He was a tall old man, with silver-streaked hair hanging to his shoulders, and wore a long robe of buckskin decorated with sun symbols. He and his people lived simply, in peeled sapling cabins, furniture made from trees of the forest, usually ingeniously designed, utilizing the natural shape of twisted limbs and roots.

'We like to stay as close to nature as possible,' Doc Hubbard said. 'We till the soil, as you have seen by our gardens and we live mostly on vegetables and herbs, but also meat on occasion when we can hunt the animals of the forest.'

There were Indians living here, too, their *tipis* scattered amongst the cramped cabins. They were of no tribe that Bryant knew but he thought they resembled Navajo or Kiowa. Hubbard called them the Tribe of the Sun, which was the name he gave his own followers. There was no church as such for worship — only a quiet, natural and tranquil glade in the forest.

But there were others who lived here, too. The man called Logan and his small gang of gun-hung men.

'Some call them outlaws,' Doc Hubbard explained, 'but we prefer to think of them as unfortunates, men who have clashed with life and do the best they can, living their own way. It may not always be according to man's laws or even the Life-Giver's, but they are human beings and we accept their foibles and presence in return for their protection.'

'From what?' asked Bryant.

Hubbard smiled slowly, spread his arms. 'Whatever danger may threaten — man; nature — they have helped us fight forest fires, floods, cyclones, wild animals. They may be called 'bad' men by people beyond the canyon country, and perhaps they are, but they are good to us in many ways and we are prepared to accept that. They appreciate the shelter we give them and the food and medical attention when they need it.'

'Ever get any converts, Doc?' Bryant asked.

'Sadly, no. And what about you, brother? You and the two men who were brought here with you? Do you have some story to tell?'

Bryant scowled, his face scaled and

raw from healing burns — some kind of herbal salve combined with, of all things, long hours stretched naked in the sun on a bed of sweet-smelling brush, was the treatment offered, plus the tribe's prayers. Surprisingly, something seemed to be doing him a power of good.

'Not much to tell, Doc. Got no money, but I've usually managed OK without much.' He sounded proud of it. 'Me and young Walt in there figured to homestead some land buttin' up against Brad McLane's B Bar M. He had other ideas. Accused us of rustlin' when we tried to return some of his cows that got mixed-in with mavericks we rounded-up.'

'Ah — that name. McLane. He does, indeed, seem in need of a life-change, but that kind of man is usually beyond such few powers as I have. He must confront the Life-Giver eventually and explain himself, and be prepared to take his punishment — for he, like all of us, must take responsibility for his actions.'

Bryant agreed with that: if he had his way, McLane would be making his confrontation with the Life-Giver as soon as Bryant was fully recovered. And the rancher could count on the company of Fletch Kirby and a couple of others, too . . .

He had no memory of his first few days here, inhabiting a world of constant pain and delirium. Then the strange treatment meted out by the tribe seemed to take effect and he began to notice his surroundings. And the strangely robed people. For a brief time he thought he had died or awakened in some sort of stop-over between Heaven and Hell.

He wasn't sure yet what awaited him here.

He got to know Hubbard and an Indian called Man-of-Storms, and some of the pale-skinned women who all seemed to be free of wrinkles or other signs of age so that it was difficult at first to pick the young from the old. But he soon learned to look at the hair, which was one giveaway, and also discovered that the older women had different symbols on their buckskin robes. These apparently changed as they advanced through various stages of the tribe.

Then one day he met Logan, the good-looking, strapping young outlaw leader who had had his men bring Bryant here with Walt Summers and Steve Macklin who were both still alive but slow to make progress towards recovery. Doc Hubbard had admitted once to Bryant that he had his doubts about Walt Summers pulling through.

'Much obliged for you bringin' me and my pard in here,' Bryant told Logan. 'Not so sure about Macklin.'

Logan grinned. 'He'll have his uses if he makes it — you all will.'

Bryant looked quizzical and, when Logan asked, told him what had happened and how he had come to be almost burned alive.

Logan nodded. 'Livin' in the forest as we do, we're all kinda leery of fire.

When we seen all that smoke we just had to take a look and make sure it wasn't gonna reach our secret trails or jump that high wall into our part of the world.'

'Were the flames that high?'

'There's scorch marks clear to the top of the wall. You were mighty lucky to fall into that cleft.'

'We were sure enough.'

'Bryant . . . ' Logan said the name thoughtfully. 'Yeah, I'm sure that was the name.'

Frank stiffened slightly on his pile of animal robes and brush. He said nothing, seeing the way the man was studying him closely now.

'You ever pack a badge — down El Paso way?'

'One time.'

Logan nodded. 'Thought it was you. Seen you down Drag Magee when he was actin'-up ornery. One shot. And Magee was king of the *pistoleros* along the border at that time.'

'I was lucky, I guess.'

'You were *fast*! That's what you were. *Damn* fast! I never seen the like before or since — and you were so sure you'd nailed him you just walked away before he started to fall.'

After a pause, Bryant said, 'Always was a good shot, right from when I was six year old and Pa gave me my first gun — an old Colt Dragoon I could hardly heft, as I recollect.'

'You sure can handle a Colt now — you got any dodgers out on you?'

'Now what kind of question is that?'

Logan shrugged, grinning. 'Figured I could get away with askin', seein' as I saved your life.'

'Well, you helped. No, no dodgers. Leastways, not now.'

Logan's grin widened. 'Done your time?'

'Let it go, Logan.'

'Whatever you say — we'll talk again. Mostly about McLane and Kirby. That interest you?'

'Could be — I'll wait and see.'

'You do that.'

Bryant hadn't seen Logan since, although he had seen the 'unfortu- nates'' camp just up the rise from the main village and hard-looking men moving about.

He spent a lot of time with Walt Summers once he was able to get around. At first, members of the tribe helped him and then he used a pair of sticks, throwing one away after a week or so and, finally, discarding the other a little later.

Walt was blind. The fire had either ruined his vision permanently or, Doc Hubbard said, it would slowly return as his body fought against its terrible wounds. The young cowboy had burns to more than eighty per cent of his body, not all deep, but every inch mighty painful. He couldn't speak and Doc wasn't sure if his throat had been damaged by the raw heat, or perhaps the vocal chords themselves had suf- fered. His face was so swollen and misshapen that Bryant had to lean close and peer hard to see the slight glint of the man's eyes deep in the folds of scarred flesh. Mostly, Walt showed signs of life through his heavily bandaged hands, giving Bryant's hand a slight pressure from time to time.

'Keep fightin', kid,' Bryant told him. 'You've got to keep fightin'.'

Steve Macklin was a different matter. The man had taken a bullet in the back, under the right shoulder and the exit wound in his chest was large and ragged. He looked pale and yellowish, eyes dark and sunken. The livid welt on his face where Brad McLane had slashed him with the quirt stood out plainly against his gravel-scarred skin.

'By God, you . . . you got one . . . helluva . . . lucky streak, Bryant!' he greeted the limping cowboy. 'Kirby was sure you'd burned to a crisp. So was I!'

'I must be about all out of luck by now,' Bryant said quietly, sitting on a log seat near the man's bunk in one of the dim cabins. 'You've got a slew of it yourself — Logan could've left you.'

'Come close to finishin' me with a

bullet, he tells me. I know why he brung me here: wants info about McLane.'

'Give it to him — you don't owe McLane a thing.'

Steve lifted a hand and touched the welt on his face. 'I owe him for this!'

'That's up to you. You and me've got somethin' to settle, too.'

'Aw, now, you seen how it was with Fletch! He's the meanest, orneriest sonofabitch ever to hit this part of Texas. I din' do what he wanted, he'd've killed me or carved me up so bad I'd have to hold my innards in with both hands . . . I aimed to quit B Bar M after we got through with you and the kid. That's gospel, Frank.'

Bryant looked back at him hard, silently.

'Look, I'm feelin' poorly right now. Lungs are on fire an' I — I keep gettin' crazy dreams, but . . . you want to git back at McLane and Kirby, I'm your . . . man. I can help you, an' I will, once I'm better.'

The man was gasping, sweat flooding down his face from his damp hairline. His eyes bulged, pleading, fear a raw, squirming thing in them.

Bryant stood shakily, looking down at Macklin. 'We'll talk later, then, Steve. You think about what you're gonna tell me — OK?'

Macklin nodded eagerly enough. 'I — I might need some protection from that Logan. He wants info about McLane, too.'

'We'll see, Steve. Just get well now.'

Macklin was shaking with fever — and maybe something else — as Bryant limped to the door and went out.

If he had to sell-out McLane and Kirby so as to get out of this with a whole hide, then he damn well would!

Like Bryant said, he owed them nothing — nothing good, leastways.

* * *

Angela McLane crossed the street, dodging nimbly through the traffic, using her sunshade to acknowledge those wagon and buckboard drivers who slowed their vehicles so she could pass. She went straight from the druggist's to Millicent Handel's Boutique, on the corner of Main and Barrow Streets.

Millicent, her light reddish hair freshly coiffured, was just finishing serving a customer and hurried things along when she saw Angela. The customer, a townswoman, with her neat parcel of fabric and thread, nodded and smiled at Angela who acknowledged with a 'Good morning, Mrs Norton', then watched the woman go out. As she suspected might happen, Mrs Norton paused just before closing the door and gave Angela a look which she interpreted, correctly, as being somewhat pitying, but mostly plain nosy.

Her mouth tightened as she realized what the look meant: the townsfolk knew, or at least suspected, that Brad was cheating on her. *The old story of* the *betrayed wife being the last to know* . . .

But her face was composed and friendly when she went to the counter where Millicent waited. The redhead was smiling, too, but there was a wariness in her eyes. Angela, somewhat angrily, recalled she had noticed the look before but had not thought it was in any way connected with her.

But, of course, Millicent Handel must have been a little on edge every time Angela entered the store, wondering if she suspected or *knew* of the affair between Millicent and Brad McLane . . .

Well, she would be in no doubt after this morning's visit.

'Good morning, Angela, you're in town early.'

'It was such a beautiful morning out at the ranch that I didn't want to waste it, so had my horse saddled and rode straight into town. I like your hair, Millie.'

She knew 'Millie' was not the redhead's favourite name and this was reflected in Millicent's face, but only briefly.

'Thank you. Can I help you with something, Angela?'

'Yes, Esther Shubridge told me your shipment of silks and guipure lace has arrived — I can't wait to see them.'

'I have them out back. Come on through and I'll lay them all out for you on the worktable.' As Millicent led the way through to the rear of the fabric-smelling shop where she employed three young townswomen, now working over treadle sewing machines, the redhead spoke over her shoulder. 'This lot cost me a pretty penny, I can tell you, Angela. I'm wondering if I did the right thing in buying them in. I mean, most of the women in this town are so unsophisticated they may not even appreciate the quality . . . '

'Well, I will,' Angela said brightly. 'I've decided to try to make some silk scarves, hand-paint them myself or dye them into my own blend of colours . . . '

Millicent stopped lifting down bolts of the multi-coloured silk and the cones of lace. '*You* are going to work with fabric and dyes?'

'Yes. I even surprised myself, but, as you know I'm not really the pioneer type, making butter, cooking, preserving fruit and vegetables, those sort of homey things.'

'But you don't have to! Brad has servants to do all that for you.'

'Exactly my point — I'm bored, Millie, bored silly some days. I've been looking for a hobby and I think I've found one.' She set down her parcel from the drugstore next to the bolts of silk that Millicent was unravelling, spreading a yard or two from each, overlapping so Angela could appreciate the various colours complementing each other.

Angela began to undo her parcel. 'Mr Rigby, the druggist, has given me a good range of dyes. See? These bottles and small tins? Scarlet, blues, greens, yellows — but I really like purple or violet and he couldn't find a ready-made lot for me but gave me this bottle of gentian violet. He says it should work well and stay fast if I add a little salt to the solution. They use it to paint on eczema. It takes weeks to fade from the skin so I'm sure it'll work satisfactorily . . . This darned cork! It's in so tight . . . '

'It's all right, Angela, I can see the colour through the glass — Don't keep trying to take it out! You might spill it on my silk and that . . . *Oh*!'

The 'Oh!' was more of a scream than an exclamation as the cork came out suddenly and the bottle jerked in Angela's hands with the release of pressure, spurting deep purple dye across Millicent's face and neck and the bodice of her clothes — and splashed in a long curving streak and large blotches across the open bolts of silk.

Then the bottle slipped completely from Angela's gloved hands and the powerful liquid glugged out soaking through the bolts of expensive silk and the cones of lace. Millicent frantically tried to claw the dye from her face, only spreading it more, befouling her hands now as well.

'Oh, dear God!' she sobbed. 'I'll be marked for weeks!'

'Just as well it wasn't the red,' Angela said on her way out, 'or you'd really look the part of a scarlet woman, Millie.' She gave a swift on-off smile, totally and unashamedly insincere. 'Sorry, dear — you'd best send the bill to Brad. I'm sure he won't mind paying.'

At the door she paused to breathe deeply of the early sunshiny air. 'Oh — what a beautiful morning it is!'

Her beaming smile brought somewhat startled looks to the faces of passers-by, all of whom were wondering what was the cause of the hysterical screaming coming from deep inside the Boutique.

5

'Howdy, Fletch'

Logan was growing impatient. He waited for Bryant to leave Doc Hubbard's cabin and, as the tall man walked towards his own quarters, almost without any signs of a limp now, he cut across, calling Frank's name.

Bryant turned, waiting for the outlaw leader. He nodded briefly.

'You're lookin' way better, Frank.'

'Feel it, too.'

'Feel like havin' a talk about Brad McLane and Fletch Kirby?'

Bryant shrugged. 'I'm talkin' about 'em all the time.' He tapped his temple. 'In here.'

'Sure. Mebbe it's time to *do* somethin', instead of just thinkin' about it.' Logan pointed to a shady elm. 'Let's go sit. Got me some fresh tobacco.'

They rolled cigarettes and lit up and smoked silently, Bryant waiting-out the other. Finally, Logan said, 'I got nothin' agin McLane, really — except the sumbitch is so damn *rich*! And me with hardly two red cents to rub together in my pockets most times.'

Bryant continued to smoke his cigarette without comment.

'I hear stories about how he treats folk, rides over 'em roughshod, kicks 'em off land he figures he wants, cuts their water by divertin' creeks to his place, sends in Kirby and his hardcases to rough' up folks he don't want around. But you're the first one I've ever met he's actually *done* somethin' to. The others cleared out, tails between their legs.'

'Folk who come to homestead are usually peaceable types, don't look for trouble. If they've got families, and most of 'em have, they just move on and look for somewhere else to settle. Likely the best move for 'em.'

'Yeah,' said Logan quickly, hitching

himself a little closer. 'That's what I mean, they all been folk who could be whipped and then hightail it for somewheres else. But not you.'

'No.'

Logan shook his head. 'Uh-uh. Not the Bryant I seen blow Drag Magee outa his boots. You're stickin' around to square things with McLane . . . least-ways Kirby, but I'd guess McLane as well.'

Frank said nothing.

'Come on! Admit it. Judas, man, don't you see the chance you've got? You want to kick butt, and you couldn't do it alone. Now you can do it — with our backin'!'

'Talkin' about you and your boys?'

'Damn right! I ain't no fool — I can see some easy pickin's here and I want to buy in.' He took a deep drag on his cigarette and looked squarely into Bryant's healing, though still-scarred, face. 'Besides, you owe me plenty. I saved your neck.'

'Well, you brought me to someone

who could,' admitted Bryant. 'I always pay my debts, Logan. I don't have to be reminded about 'em.'

'Aw, hell, I'm just spellin' it out so's there ain't no misunderstandin's.' He punched Bryant lightly on one shoulder, grinning. 'I know you got a code. Heard about it before you squared up to Magee. Fact is, I stayed on in El Paso to get a look at you. Didn't really believe all I'd heard. But let's talk about the future, not the past — what you got in mind?'

Bryant stubbed out his cigarette butt against the sole of the moccasin Hubbard's women had given him. He glanced at Logan.

'Steve's the man knows about McLane. He's comin' good, Doc tells me. Another few days and he'll be spry enough to take notice.'

'How about your pard? That kid, Summers?'

Frank's face straightened. 'Funeral service is at sundown,' he said in clipped tones. 'Walt died last night.'

Elation filled Logan's chest although he covered it by frowning and shaking his head, lips pursed. 'Mighty sorry to hear that. Guess you've got more reason than ever to go after McLane now.'

Bryant's eyes were cold: he had detected the eagerness and false compassion in Logan's tone. 'Kirby's the one I want — he set that fire. McLane can get in line.'

'But you'll get round to him when you're ready — and me and the boys'll be waitin' to lend a hand!'

Frank Bryant didn't even say 'so long' when Logan stood and moved off. He was staring at his scarred hands, working the fingers, frowning when he saw just how stiff they were.

Well, if they couldn't yet work a trigger or gun hammer, they could still pound a man into the ground . . .

★   ★   ★

'*Angela! Angela!* Where the hell are you . . . ?'

79

She was in the small study attached to her room, writing some letters. McLane's heavy tread shook the stairs as he pounded his way up to the top floor of the ranch house. She could imagine his reddened, sweaty face, contorted into an ugly bad-tempered look. Too, she could imagine the staff downstairs scattering to make themselves scarce, far from where the rancher was roaring for his wife.

They all knew better than to be within reach when Brad McLane was out of sorts.

Angela made no attempt to stop writing, didn't even glance up when she heard him enter her bedroom.

She knew she ought to be all knotted up inside, shaking perhaps, dreading the confrontation. In fact, she was rather looking forward to it now — at long last she had things out in the open and . . .

'Are you deaf or something! Dammit, I've been calling out to you!'

'I heard you — in fact, I'd say most

of the county heard you.'

That stopped him in his tracks as he took a couple of long strides into the room. He narrowed his eyes as dust from his ride back from town jarred loose from the shoulders of his jacket.

'So! This is how it's going to be!'

'How what's going to be? Look, Brad, just let me finish this letter to my Aunt Claire and then I'll happily discuss whatever it is that's upset you this time.'

He took that extra step and reached out and tore the page from under her pen, screwing it up and hurling it into a corner. She looked at him coldly.

'Don't be so childish! For Heaven's sake, what is it that's bothering you?'

'Oh? You don't know? The *hell* you don't!' He reached into a jacket pocket and brought out a crumpled sheet of paper and shook it in her face. '*This* is what's the matter! This bill for almost seven hundred dollars' worth of imported Chinese silk and French lace!'

The woman frowned. 'I never bought that . . . '

He snapped and slapped her. She almost fell out of the chair and, when she straightened, eyes brimming, one side of her face red and white with the shape of his hand and fingers, she jutted her small jaw and squared her shoulders.

'Where did she give it to you? In town? Or down by the river at Tall Cedar Bend?'

He frowned, hand half-raised to strike her again, but she stepped back and picked up a paper-knife, holding it protectively in front of her.

'I'll use it if I have to, Brad!'

She was surprised at how calm she felt and she saw it had its effect on McLane. He looked mighty wary now, nostrils flaring as he drew in deep breaths, steadying himself down.

'So — you knew! *That's* why you threw that dye all over Millicent's silk! She said you did it deliberately, but I doubted her! My God, Angela, I've never seen you like this before!'

'Get used to it, Brad. I know about you and Millie Handel and while I probably should be ashamed of what I did, I'm not! I feel pretty darn good about it! What d'you think of that?'

His frown deepened. 'I . . . dunno just what to make of it. I'm thinking that if you'd do something like that to Millicent, what will you do to me?'

She smiled slowly. 'Oh? You haven't noticed yet?'

Alarm squirmed across his face. 'What? What've you done to me? How . . . ?'

She smiled. 'What does it matter? You're no longer interested in me. Why, only the other night at supper I mentioned that you never come to my bed now. Of course, keeping up with *two* women might well be beyond a man of your age . . . '

'Dammit, I'm only forty-three! If you think I can't handle more than one woman at a time — '

She arched her eyebrows. 'Forty-three? Why that's almost five years older than you led me to believe you are. I would've thought you were certainly . . . virile . . . enough to 'handle' more than one woman, as you put it, perhaps there's something happening to you. Something — '

'There's nothing happening to me!' he roared, almost beside himself that she would throw doubts on his virility. 'By God, up in Canada they used to call me the Stallion and — '

'Canada? That's the first I knew you'd even been to Canada, let alone build some sort of a reputation there.'

She could see she had shaken him: he had let something slip he hadn't meant to and she saw the meanness come back into his face, pushing aside his anger. Instinctively, she stepped back, getting a tighter grip on the handle of the paper-knife.

'Hasn't Millie noticed your ardour falling away?' she asked quietly, as he lunged towards her.

It was like a pail of ice water dashing him in the face. He stopped, blinking.

'Wh — ? Oh, you *bitch*! My food! I've been complaining to that damn Mexican cook how salty and spicy my food's been lately. She told me you were trying out new recipes.' He threw up his hands. '*Cherrisssst*! Who the hell ever named you Angel? You — you're a she-devil! You put something in my food! Something that . . . '

He became inarticulate and she would have taken the opportunity to leave but he was between her and the door.'

'Well, it was probably bromide or saltpetre — they're only temporary,' he said finally, speaking as if to himself. 'I'll come good again . . . I'll . . . '

'Perhaps it will be too late, Brad. I mean, poor Millie probably thinks because of all those purple and violet splotches on her face and bosom that she's lost her attraction and you're losing interest in her.'

She wasn't ready for him when he suddenly slapped the knife out of her hand, twisted her wrist and her arm, bringing her to her knees, sobbing in pain.

'You just might be righter than you know, you evil bitch! But that doesn't get you off the hook! You think you've had some kind of revenge? Some kind of victory? Let me tell you something, you female Satan, I can write the book on getting even! If I want to have an affair, I'll have it! I won't ask your permission and you'll be here whenever I decide I want you. And you'll *do just like I say!* No ifs, no buts, no arguments. I won't kill you if you give me a fight, but, by hell, I might make you so unattractive to any man that even the Border whorehouses won't take you!'

He thrust his face close to hers. 'You savvy me? You understand?' He shook her until her teeth rattled and her legs would barely hold her, her heart smashing wildly against her chest. 'You're mine and you'll stay mine until *I* decide to dump you, where and when and how. It'll be all up to me. I won't keep you locked up — you can go for your usual rides, anywhere you wish — but there'll be someone either with you or watching you and they'll make sure you return home — *here!* — every day.'

He threw her to the floor and placed a boot across her slim white neck, no real weight behind it yet. He leaned down, teeth bared.

'You're Mrs Bradford McLane for just as long as I want. You think you can mess with my life? Lady, I'm gonna make your life *hell*! And there's not one goddamn thing you can do about it!'

★ ★ ★

Steve Macklin was progressing well. He was able to sit up now and spend some time in the sun.

Bryant came to see him often and this day, the sun bright and burning, Steve was propped up in a makeshift armchair made from the fork of a tree and nailed-on burlap with rawhide support straps, and was relaxed and dozing, but woke when a shadow came between him and the sun.

He lifted a hand to shade his eyes, saw that it was Bryant. The tall man was looking much fitter now, had gained a sun tan and put on some weight. He squatted beside Macklin's chair, rolled a cigarette and lit it.

Walt Summers had been buried over a week ago and Frank was anxious to start something moving to avenge his young pard's death. It wasn't so much that Walt had died, but the manner of his dying which brought the dead coldness filling Bryant now. Badly burned, blinded, mute, not even able to croak any last words or state a last wish — it oughtn't to have happened to any man and it stuck in Bryant's craw like nothing else had in all his thirty-four years. He felt responsible for having brought Walt to this neck of the woods in the first place.

'Time for you to talk to me, Steve.'

Macklin made no pretence that he

didn't understand what Bryant was saying, merely sighed and nodded.

'What you want to know, Frank?'

'Whatever you know about McLane — and Fletch Kirby.'

'Fletch is easy — he's about the orneriest bastard I've ever known. Most folk who know him figure the same. Bully from way back, laps up violence and seein' others suffer like a cat laps milk. Bastard made the claim once, when he caught some homesteader cuttin' the bob-wire, that he could make the man confess he was put up to it by a feller named Curtin, leader of the sod-busters at the time. 'I can make you scream so long you'll figure it's just ten minutes short of forever, you sumbitch!' is what he told that feller and by hell he done it. Only time I've ever looked at someone all tore up and threw-up . . . '

'I can savvy Kirby: I've run into his kind before.'

Steve shook his head. 'No you ain't — ain't but one piece of dog-shit like

Fletch Kirby and the damn world can be almighty thankful for that!'

'All I need to know is his habits, where he rides on the B Bar M and so on.'

Steve snorted, winced and clutched at his chest. He blew out his cheeks. 'Hell, I better watch doin' that! Ah, Fletch does pretty much what he likes an' McLane lets him. He's one of his top bodyguards and — '

'McLane's got more'n one body-guard?'

'Hell, yeah! Half a dozen. I was one for a while but I din' like ridin' agin sod-busters with families. 'Cause Fletch always dragged the families into it. Beat or raped the women, or both. Kids — he used to get a kick outa makin' them watch while he worked on the old man or the mother.'

Bryant's face was grim. 'Move on from Kirby — he's already dead. Just don't know it yet.'

Macklin looked at him sharply, studying the hard face with its fading scars and slowly he nodded. 'I b'lieve you're the man to do it if you get half a chance.'

'I'll make my chance, Steve.'

'OK — McLane, well, he's somethin' of a mystery. No one even knows where he comes from for sure, 'cept back East someplace. Turned up with the woman one time, all set to be married, bought up some land, hauled in all the fancy timber and fireplace from somewheres back East and built the big house. Brought in a hardcase crew with Fletch Kirby runnin' 'em and turned 'em loose in the county to clear it out of sodbusters and small-time ranches. Bought the law and half the town, poured money into businesses, won over the folk by puttin' on big picnic meetin's and dances.' He spread his arms. 'Moved right in and took over is the quickest way of sayin' it.'

Bryant had seen it all before, had himself fallen victim once up in Nevada, kicked off a silver claim because a rich and powerful man got greedy and wanted his lease when he learned Bryant was getting a good return of silver for every ton of ore dug and crushed. They put a price on his head, that time, framed him, and he had to clear the territory. One day he'd go back, though. That man was richer and more powerful than ever now, but Bryant had learned one important thing in the intervening years: the more a man owned, the richer he became, the more vulnerable he was . . . because he had so much more to lose.

'Tell me what you know about Mrs McLane,' he said suddenly, and Steve looked at him sharply.

'Well, now, she's a mighty interesting subject . . . '

★ ★ ★

Angela was sick of it, this being under endless surveillance. It didn't matter what she did, there was always someone watching her — Kirby himself, or Pink, or Carlos, or that gunslinger who had turned up one day and seemed to know

Brad, the lantern-jawed man with the blank eyes he had hired as a bodyguard. The one they called The Widowmaker.

It made her shudder just to look at him . . .

Now she decided to try to escape. Long before she had had her suspicions about Brad's infidelity confirmed, she had been able to ride anywhere she wanted and there were trails she had explored and places she had found that seemed free of cattle — which meant that the cowboys had either never been there, or if they had and failed to locate B Bar M cows, they hadn't come back.

Today was the day when she would try to escape this suffocating life Brad had thrust upon her. She had crammed spare clothing and a few belongings into her saddle-bags after he had promised only last night at supper, to make her life even more hellish, after he had come back from town slightly drunk, a smudge on his shirt front that she knew was most likely some of Millie

93

Handel's face powder. Perhaps the effects of the bromide hadn't yet worn off completely — maybe that accounted for his foul mood.

Now, somewhere behind her, she knew Kirby followed and maybe there were others of his men, too, but she had to risk it. Mind, she would have preferred that Kirby wasn't within twenty miles of her this day, but it had just worked out that way, and she knew she had to make her attempt while she still had the courage.

She had a good rapport with the palomino: the horse liked her and she had trained the gelding to respond instantly to her signals. As usual, Kirby was well back, aloof and confident she would not make any attempt to escape. With the bandages off his face, Kirby looked more frightening than ever. The doctor had been unable to set his crushed nose very well and it seemed like a twisted lump of rubber separating his high cheekbones, the stretched skin pulling up the ramrod's top lip so that some of his yellowed teeth showed in a kind of constant sneer. It did not add to his looks and, if anything, he was meaner than before that day he had had his run-in with the man called Frank Bryant.

Of course, Bryant was dead now, like most men who tangled with Fletch Kirby . . .

She stopped by a stream and knelt to drink, using the motion to turn and look behind. Yes, there he was, sitting his horse casually way back on the ridge, one heel hooked on the saddle-horn while he twisted up a cigarette. She would never have a better chance than right now!

She mounted without hurry, then drove home her silver spurs, wrenched the startled horse's head around and plunged the animal into the stream. Water flew in silver fans and the palomino grunted and heaved into midstream, swimming strongly for the far bank. Angela looked over her shoulder: Kirby was only now starting to leave the ridge — and he had yet to ride back to the trail which dropped below the point where he had been waiting, for he had left it for the vantage point of a projecting tongue of rock higher up-slope.

Her heart was pounding and she lashed at the straining horse with her rein ends. If only she could get across and into that brush and the timber beyond, she could ride into a small hidden canyon she had discovered by chance and —

Her heart plunged to the pit of her stomach as two riders came out of the brush on the far side. Instinctively, she started to haul rein and then one of the men lifted a rifle and called, 'Come on across, ma'am. I'm pretty sure you'd rather do that than have me shoot that fine-lookin' hoss out from under you.'

It was the dead man — the man she *thought* was dead, Frank Bryant! She had never seen the other man before but she knew who he was by description: Logan, an outlaw . . .

She turned and looked back, saw Kirby coming hell for leather towards the stream and a rider coming out of the trees to join him. *Pink!*

My God, what a mess she was in.

She snapped her head up as she heard Bryant's rifle lever clash. 'Ma'am, I won't wait any longer!'

The Winchester was at his shoulder and she made her decision, rode the palomino across. It heaved up the bank, shaking water from its coat as Logan moved in and smiled at her even as he expertly whipped a loop of rope about her wrists.

'Let me go!' she hissed, but the words were drowned in the whiplash of Bryant's rifle and she stood in the stirrups in time to see Kirby's horse go down, tail over tip, tossing the ramrod heavily to the ground. He skidded and rolled, brought up against a rock and lay still.

Pink was shooting back with his sixgun and she watched Bryant deliberately bead the man, his shot blowing

Pink out of the saddle. He flopped and bounced in the dust and ended with his head hanging over the low bank into the stream. The water was tinged red around his floating hair.

Bryant put his horse back across the stream, rifle covering Kirby as the man sat up groggily, shaking his head slowly, blinking.

'Don't make any stupid moves.'

Kirby started at the voice, froze briefly, then narrowed his eyes and stared incredulously at Bryant. He moved a hand towards his gun butt and jumped when Bryant put a bullet between his spread legs, dust and grit spurting.

As the lever jacked another shell into the rifle's breech, Kirby pressed back against the rock and slowly raised his hands shoulder high.

Bryant rode right up so close that his horse's forelegs were almost touching Kirby. He grinned coldly, and placed the hot muzzle of the rifle between Kirby's staring eyes.

'Howdy, Fletch — long time, no see.'

6

Pay Up!

Brad McLane stomped up the stairs to the top floor of the ranch house, looked once more in Angela's rooms, knowing she was not there, but compelled to look anyway.

He slammed out, went to the window in his own bedroom and yanked the curtains aside hard enough to tear the fabric. The western sky was beginning to take on that mellow, pale-orange look that heralded sundown. He snatched his field-glasses from the peg on the wall, adjusted focus.

He raked the countryside with all its shadows and even raised the lenses to take in the slopes of the hogback well beyond the ranch yard. *No sign of her! No sign of her, nor Kirby or Pink either!*

The hell had happened? They were *always* back by this time. If that bitch had been stupid enough to try to run — no. She wouldn't get more than a few yards: he knew he could trust Kirby to stop her in her tracks, even if it meant shooting that damn expensive palomino out from under her. Anyway, Pink was out there and he was no slouch, either. No, she couldn't have run off, so something else must have happened. An accident? Could be, but one of them would have gotten word back to the ranch by now.

'What ... the ... hell?' he said aloud, adjusting focus swiftly as the lenses picked up some movement on the edge of the deep shadow of a draw at the base of the hogback. No one should be coming in from that side. 'Hell almighty!'

He tossed the field-glasses on to his bed and lunged out of the room, skidding at the top of the stairs, leaping down wildly.

McLane plunged out on to the porch

100

and yelled at the first man he saw in the yard, which happened to be Carlos, just coming out of the men's privy at the rear of the bunkhouse.

'*Si, señor?*' Carlos said, playing up his Mexican heritage. Some days he did this, using a lot of Spanish in his speech and even accenting any English words. Other times he spoke American flawlessly.

'Someone riding in!' McLane called, pointing. 'Riding double. Looks like one's hurt! Get out there . . . fast!'

Carlos leapt on to the bare back of a horse tethered to the hickory rail outside the bunkhouse and spurred away in the direction McLane was pointing. The rancher watched him for a moment and then began pacing the porch, back and forth, back and forth.

The riders looked like two men to him. If that meant Angela had been hurt . . . No! He damn well didn't want that! He wanted her alive and well, fully aware of her punishment and how he was in control, how she was at *his* mercy and whims.

He was breathing hard through pinched nostrils when Carlos came riding back, leading the second horse. McLane saw the man draped across the horse's withers now, head down, obviously dead, the other sagging in the saddle. He swallowed and felt his face pale.

It was Fletch Kirby and there was blood all over him, especially on his hands and at his knees!

There was a high, keening sound and McLane began to shake for it was a sound he had never heard before, one he had never thought he would *ever* hear.

It was Kirby — sobbing in extreme pain!

Carlos hauled rein at the foot of the steps. He looked yellowish and sick.

'Pink is dead, *señor*. Fletch — well, he has been destroyed. Both knees have been shot out and a bullet has been put through each of his hands. The back of his shirt has been burned away, his flesh — ' He grimaced and spat.

'Christ, the Indians haven't cut loose again, have they?'

Carlos shook his head. 'I think not, señor.' He fumbled in his pocket and brought out a piece of bloodstained, crumpled paper. There was writing on it. He handed it to McLane. 'This was pinned to the front of Fletch's shirt.'

McLane took it slowly, surprised to find his hand was trembling a little. He looked at his ramrod. If he hadn't known who he was he would never have recognized him. Not that his face was battered any more than it had been when he had left. It had simply — crumpled. There was no other way to describe it.

All the features seemed to have slid out of place, were hanging loosely, the eyes glazed and dead-looking — except for the tears that welled out of them. The twisted, smashed mouth moved as he sucked in a shuddering breath and released it as a whine like that of a kicked puppy.

'Who did this?' McLane whispered hoarsely, still holding the paper unread. 'Who *did* this!'

He was surprised to see Kirby's head lift an inch and the tear-filled eyes rested on the rancher's face and for a moment there was recognition there. Fletch made a guttural sound and McLane frowned at Carlos.

'You make out what he said?'

Carlos's eyes were wide. 'It — it sound like he say . . . *Bryant*!'

McLane took an involuntary step back. 'Bryant!' he whispered. 'But the man's dead! Burned alive . . . ' His hands tightened and he became aware of the paper again, smoothed it out and turned it so the amber glow of the fast-setting sun washed across the blood and dirt and creases.

He could just make out the crudely printed words:

$20,000 delivered to Broken Rock by noon Tuesday or you get her left ear nailed to your door — each

day you get a different piece of your woman till you pay up.

'I don't think he'll pay.'

Bryant looked up sharply from where he bent over Angela's lap as she sat on a log and he fumbled to untie her bonds.

She was pale and drawn in the flickering light of the camp-fire outside the cabin used by Bryant in the settlement deep in the Breaks.

'He doesn't, you're goin' to lose an ear.'

Fear showed as she rubbed her wrists, marked deeply by the rope that had tied her hands to the saddlehorn on the ride back in here. She had been blindfolded as an extra precaution and she still felt a little disoriented.

'I . . . have no doubt you will take it, Mr Bryant — any man who can do what you did to Fletch Kirby . . . ' Her voice trailed as she saw his face and the narrowing of his eyes.

'Fletch is an animal.'

'And what does it make you, that you

did such horrors to him?' She sounded indignant.

He shrugged. 'I'll answer for it when I meet my Maker.'

'The terrible thing is you are *willing* to do just that. You have no remorse for what you did.'

'About as much as Fletch had for burnin' young Walt — blindin' him and makin' him mute into the bargain. Chris'sake, woman, he was only just past twenty!'

She was silent for a time. 'Yes, it was terrible but what you did to Fletch Kirby was even more terrible.'

'I hope so — I don't want him to die yet. That way it'll all be over for him. He's got to suffer some, same as Walt. He's crippled now and I feel good about it.'

She shook her head, sighing. 'I think you are even more terrible than Fletch Kirby, Mr Bryant!'

'Let it go, will you!' he snapped, and suddenly she knew he was not really satisfied with what he had done. He had gone through with it because he believed he had to, not because he wanted to. He felt it was his duty.

She was surprised to realize that maybe he even felt sorry for Kirby. But it wouldn't change anything: Bryant's young pard had died horribly at Kirby's hands, and Bryant's code dictated that Walt had to be fully avenged and if that meant soaking his own hands in blood and sadism, then Bryant was quite willing to accept responsibility for his actions.

It took a tough man to do that, she admitted silently. Tough and, in his own way, righteous.

'Now I am to suffer to make my husband pay for his part in your friend's death,' she said curtly. 'And you intend to profit from it!'

Bryant smiled crookedly. 'Mebbe I will and mebbe I won't. I just want to shake McLane up, get him jumpy after seein' what happened to Kirby.'

Angela frowned. 'You are a strange man, Frank Bryant. You claim the money means little to you . . . '

'It don't mean a thing one way or the other.'

'I don't believe you!'

He shrugged. 'I don't care if McLane pays — but I dunno why he wouldn't when he has such a beautiful wife. But if he doesn't, I'll find some other way to shake him up.'

'By sending him pieces of me!'

The crooked smile widened. 'We'll wait till Tuesday and see.'

Doc Hubbard sent one of his women across to ask if Angela could sleep in the women's quarters.

'We will watch her carefully, if that is what you wish, Mr Bryant,' said the middle-aged woman he knew as Star. She was fine-looking and pleasant, softly spoken. 'The good doctor does not allow prisoners in his camp.'

'Sorry, Star. I need to hold Angela for a few days, maybe longer.'

'Then she must have the freedom of the camp while she is here. Bondage will not be tolerated. She will not leave, she does not know where she is. Her horse is kept in our hidden canyon with our own animals. From what I've heard I would say she does not know the wilds very well, so even if she were to find a way out . . . '

Bryant sighed and held up a hand. 'All right, all right! Just see she doesn't wander off . . . I mean you no harm, ma'am. It's just your bad luck you happen to be married to that . . . scum.'

'Yes — it is rather unfortunate,' she replied, surprising him and the woman. 'How did you come to marry someone like McLane?'

'Swept off my feet. Young and impressionable, dazzled by his worldliness and wealth. By the way, 'McLane' is *my* name, not his. Part of our . . . pact . . . was that we use my name.'

Star looked startled and Bryant frowned. 'You gave him your name and not the other way around?'

Angela nodded. 'It was part of the attraction, you see. The man of mystery. He told me there was a reason for it

109

and I worried at him until he admitted he had come by his wealth through theft, although he hastened to add that the people he stole it from had acquired it by illegal means.'

'Double-crossed someone, sounds like.'

'I don't know the details, but I believed him and still do.'

'What's his real name. He tell you?'

She hesitated, then nodded. 'He told me a name, because I pestered him about it, but it wasn't the right one. Only later did I happen across one of his papers, his previous marriage certificate. He was a widower when I met him, you see, and the name was different. But I believe it is his real one — Roberto Rivelle. It didn't sound like the kind of name a man would make up. It is a French spelling, I'm told, of the English 'Revell'.'

Bryant frowned and then Star, growing restless, took Angela's elbow and glanced at him. He nodded and Angela was led away towards the long cabin of the women of the Tribe of the Sun.

'Where's she goin'?' asked Logan quickly, as he came out of the cabin he now shared with Bryant.

Bryant explained, but the outlaw leader didn't seem happy.

'She's gotta stay till the ransom's paid! I don't care what happens after that, but she's gotta stay until it's paid!'

Bryant didn't tell him that Angela thought her husband would refuse to pay up . . .

★ ★ ★

Tuesday seemed a long time coming and when it did, it was raining.

But Bryant, Logan and Ned Nudge waited under an overhang of rock that looked down on the Broken Rock rendezvous, fingering their guns.

'He better damn well pay up!' gritted Nudge, and Logan nodded, grim-faced.

He was in it for the money and nothing else. Bryant had told him he and his men could keep it. He just wanted to test McLane to find out if Angela was the chink in the man's armour. Maybe he didn't like using the woman, but he saw it as the *only* way to get under McLane's skin now.

Or he *had* seen it that way. But he had had a chance only yesterday to ask her if she really believed that McLane would not pay the ransom and she had nodded.

'Brad and I do not get along. He has been unfaithful and I am not the type of person who can sit still under such treatment. We . . . had an argument and he was . . . brutal. I had no cause not to believe he would carry out every threat he made to me. I was trying to escape, as you saw, when you intervened.'

'Yeah — that's what got me thinkin' maybe you're right, he won't pay.'

'And will you still.. take my ear?'

He hadn't answered, walked away and left her wondering. Fact was, he was wondering himself.

'Rider!' hissed Ned Nudge suddenly,

and pointed, rain clattering against his stiff slicker.

They saw the blurred rider down there, making his way up the muddy trail to the splintered boulder known as Broken Rock. Clad as he was in a slicker and tugged-down hat they could not tell who he was, but he did have a canvas sack slung from his saddle-horn.

Nudge turned his head and grinned at Logan, showing large stained and decayed teeth. 'Jackpot!'

They watched the man ride up to the broken boulder and look around carefully before taking the sodden sack from the saddlehorn and placing it in a hollow in the shattered rock. They saw then he was holding a sixgun just underneath his slicker.

'It's that damn Mex gunslinger!' Nudge said, lifting his rifle.

Bryant pushed the weapon down. 'He'll keep. Let him ride out.'

The big outlaw was reluctant, but at a nod from Logan he lowered the gun and eased the hammer down. Carlos looked around warily and backed his horse up until he reached the edge of the timber again. Then he wheeled and they heard him galloping back down the trail.

They waited a while before riding down to the hollow in Broken Rock. Nudge stood in his stirrups, reached up and pulled out the sack. Something metallic clinked inside and his ugly grin widened.

'Hey! Looks like we got us some real *dinero* at last, boss!'

Bryant held out his hand. 'Give it here!'

At the sharp edge in Bryant's voice, Ned Nudge's jaw jutted and he moved his rifle up but Logan pushed it aside.

'Let him have it. It was his idea.'

Ned scowled, glaring at Bryant, clearly unhappy.

They rode back to the overhang and dismounted and Bryant untied the drawstrings, reaching inside, feeling the cold round discs of metal. But when he pulled out his hand and spilled them on to the ground they glinted like silver — but were only iron washers.

Nudge, savagely angry, snatched the bag, upended it and poured out a large pile of the washers. There was a piece of paper there, too — the same note Bryant had pinned to Kirby's shirt.

He smoothed it out and saw a big cross in red ink over the ransom demand.

Underneath in the same red ink was a short message from Brad McLane:

Keep her. She's all yours. Feed the bits and pieces to the coyotes.

7

Hidden Riches

The rain had stopped.

Doc Hubbard was waiting near the women's cabin when they returned to the camp. He studied their faces closely and watched Ned Nudge rake his hard eyes over Angela who was with Star and Lady, learning how to clean and work a butter churn.

She straightened from washing the leather plunger and her lithe body tensed as Bryant and the others dismounted. Logan nodded and even smiled faintly but she could see the tension in him, and the other two.

'He didn't pay,' she said quietly, and Frank shook his head.

'Sent a bag of lousy washers!' snarled Ned. 'You know what that means, sweetheart.'

He stepped forward, a hand going to his hunting knife. Bryant snapped his name and Hubbard stepped forward, holding up a hand, palm-out.

'You know better than that, brother.'

Ned glared. 'We made a promise — McLane din' pay up, now we gotta show him we ain't foolin' around! Step aside, Doc. She's due to lose an ear!'

Logan said nothing and didn't interfere when Bryant grabbed Ned's arm, spun him around and rammed his six gun's muzzle hard into his ribs. He made sure the big man heard the hammer cock.

'Leave her be, Ned.'

Their faces were inches apart and Nudge was breathing heavily. Bryant increased the pressure of the gun and suddenly Ned's lips tightened and he took his hand off his knife, stepping back.

'He's got the money! Why can't we make him pay?'

'There are other ways.'

Ned snorted. 'I ain't got a lot of faith

in what you say, Bryant! You made a threat, now you ain't gonna carry it out. You ain't my kinda man!'

'I'll try not to lose much sleep over that, Ned.' Bryant jerked his head. 'Do us a favour and take care of the horses, OK?'

Ned Nudge didn't like it, but Bryant made the request sound reasonable and Logan nodded. Muttering, Nudge took up the mounts' reins and moved away towards the corrals. Bryant holstered his gun, turning to the pale-faced Angela.

'Your ears are safe. And the rest of you.'

She almost smiled. 'I'm glad to hear it. What happened at Broken Rock?'

Bryant told her and the others, showed them the note. Angela looked kind of sick. 'I didn't think he hated me that much.' She gave an involuntary shiver. 'It's — awful!'

Star put her arm about her shoulder and led her away with Lady coming up to take Angela's other arm.

'This McLane sounds an evil man,' opined Doc Hubbard. He watched the women take Angela into the cabin. 'She apparently exacted her own kind of revenge for his — er — extra-marital transgressions. This would appear to be his way of getting his own back.' Hubbard shook his head slowly. 'I have never met this McLane, but his response to your ransom demand sounds pretty much in keeping with what I've heard about him.'

Logan turned his gaze to Bryant. 'Kind of stymies us, don't it?'

'Like I told Ned, there are other ways.'

'Like what?'

'I'll have to give it some thought — Steve must know a lot more about McLane . . . '

As they moved away towards the cabin where Macklin sat in his tree-fork easy-chair, Doc Hubbard said quietly, 'The Bible says *Thou Shalt Not Kill*, but a Hebrew scholar I know assures me the translation should be *Thou*

Shalt Not Commit Murder. There is a fine distinction, brothers. Please give it some thought. Sin demands large payment — in full.'

Logan and Bryant didn't answer and took whatever thoughts they had on the subject to Steve Macklin in silence. Steve wasn't surprised at McLane's response to the ransom note. 'Would've figured somethin' was wrong if he'd paid up — But twenty thousand is small change to him.'

Logan nodded. 'Just told Frank that.'

'How do you know? Sure, McLane's got a big place, thousands of cattle, but his ready cash might be tied up.'

'We can take it in cows,' Logan growled, put out at not getting his hands on that twenty thousand.

'McLane would have the law on your tail before you could reach a market,' Macklin said. 'You can't cross that sonuver. Only way to get what you want from him is to take it, then sprout wings and fly away, a *long* way away!'

'Thought you said he's got lots of

guards and pays fightin' wages?' snapped Logan, still in a bad mood.

'He does. Never said it'd be easy, but takin's the only way. And you'd have to use plenty of force. More'n I see round here.'

'What's it matter now?' Logan said. 'McLane don't care about the woman. We can't use her for a lever no more.'

'Steve, you once hinted that McLane was sittin' on a pile of cash. I never picked up on it then but it's come back to me now. Did you mean it, or were you just talkin'?'

Steve looked vaguely uncomfortable, shrugged. 'Well, Frank, there was a rumour goin' around B Bar M and had been for a long time. No one could say for sure, but there was always this story that McLane didn't trust banks and was sittin' on a fortune . . . '

'Anyone ever see the stash?' Logan asked hopefully.

'Not that I ever heard,' Steve told him.

'Why don't we ask the woman?' Frank suggested, and Logan grinned,

121

started back towards the women's cabin, but Bryant grabbed his arm. 'I'll do the askin'.'

Logan glowered. 'Why you?'

'Just leave it to me, Logan.'

'Listen,' the outlaw gritted, shaking his arm free. 'You seem to be tryin' to take over here!'

'No — just tryin' to get the best result easiest way possible.'

'How'll we know what she tells you? You could say there's nothin' doin', then grab what you can for yourself.'

'If I was interested in money, I could,' admitted Frank. 'But I'm only interested because of what it can do to McLane by takin' it off him. You and your men, and the woman, can have the damn money — it's McLane I'm after.'

Logan watched sullenly as Bryant walked away across the slope to the big cabin, spoke to a woman at the door who went inside. Soon after, Angela McLane appeared and seemed a little red-eyed, shaken badly by her husband's note, no doubt.

Ned Nudge joined Logan, saw his boss's face and asked what was wrong.

'Nothin' yet — but we keep a close eye on Bryant.'

'He's a straight-shooter,' dropped in Steve, but the others only gave him cold looks.

* * *

Frank and Angela walked down by the stream, found a quiet grove of white oak and sat down on a deadfall. She waited patiently while Bryant made a cigarette and lit up.

'You want to leave?' he asked unexpectedly, his words bringing her head around with a jerk.

A slight frown appeared between her eyes as she looked him up and down. 'You want to turn me loose?'

He shrugged. 'Can't use you as a lever on McLane and I got no real stomach for kidnappin', just keepin' you here.'

'Well! You see, Frank Bryant, I was

trying to escape when you and Logan abducted me. I have no money, Brad would never give me any — oh, he paid for things I wanted, but he made sure I could never get my hands on more than a couple of dollars at a time. So, in a way, I'm quite used to being held hostage.'

He seemed uncomfortable. 'Then you're actually better off away from him?'

'God, yes! I would never voluntarily go back to him — but he could come after me, you know.'

'Not accordin' to that note.'

'He would have written that in anger as a way of deliberately spoiling your plans. But he is very possessive and when he stops to think, he might just get all his gunslingers and hardcases together and come looking.'

She glanced back up the slope to the camp. 'These are good people, Frank. I wouldn't want to bring trouble upon them — yet, I believe I could be happy here. I feel a . . . peace and a . . . calm here that I've never felt anywhere else. I enjoy learning the small things Star and Lady have been teaching me. Never thought I would, but, here — well, it seems *right*, somehow.'

'You want to stay here, then?'

'I think I do. But at the same time, I wouldn't want Brad to bring his men here.'

'He doesn't know of this place. Has never been able to find out if it actually existed even, accordin' to Steve.'

'That's true but, just the same, I'm not sorry you took me away from Brad, you know. And I'm willing to help you even the score you have to settle with him, if I can do anything.'

He dragged on his cigarette, looked up from the glowing end into her face. 'Is it true he keeps a lot of cash in the house? Or somewhere on B Bar M?'

She smiled. 'So Steve told you about the rumour.'

'Is that all it is?'

She picked up a stem of grass and picked the seeds off one by one before she replied. 'It's not just a rumour, Frank.'

Bryant stiffened. 'You sure?'

'I've seen some of it. The money I mean.'

His breath whistled softly between his teeth. 'Much?'

'He claims in excess of — You won't believe me.'

'Try me.'

She took a deep breath, met and held his gaze. 'He claims he has access to more than a hundred thousand dollars at any given time.'

* * *

That night, Bryant didn't sleep well.

He kept tossing and turning on his bunk, thinking about what the woman had told him. But mostly he couldn't shake off that figure — A *hundred thousand dollars!* It was a dream. Some Western banks operated on less capital than that!

It was a tremendous amount of

money for the day and age, an unimaginable amount to most people.

He had not told Logan.

Yes, he had said in answer to the young outlaw's query, it seemed that McLane did have a stash of money hidden somewhere, the woman was sure of that. But he lied and said she didn't know how much or, leastways, said McLane never mentioned a figure. It would be leaked soon enough, he reckoned.

He had been too stunned to even ask any questions after she had told him. But she went on to say that McLane had been a little drunk, in a boastful mood, had shown her a leather valise stuffed with money.

'Ten thousand bucks in there in nice crisp notes,' he had told her, words slurring slightly. 'Ah! You impressed, huh? Well, how impressed would you be if I told you I can lay my hands on ten times that much any time of the day or night! Huh? How about that?'

She had been impressed and who

could blame her. Of course, McLane had not elaborated, locked up the valise in the big ranch safe. She knew the rest of the cash was not in there, but she had believed him, somehow, had been married to him long enough to know when he was just boasting or telling the truth.

'Where would he get his hands on that much money? You said he reckoned he'd stolen it but where from?'

She didn't know, but he had said that if ever he had to run for his life, he had more than enough to start over again. He'd even told Angela that he had picked this part of Texas to start his 'empire' because, if the need arose, he could be in Mexico in a few days — either to make a new life there, or use it as a stepping off place to anywhere else in the world.

'Did he give you any more details?'

'I asked him. He was vague and enigmatic, but couldn't leave it alone. It was as if he wanted to tell me but couldn't quite bring himself to do so

— something was holding him back.'

'Self-preservation,' Bryant said, and she glanced at him sharply and agreed.

'Exactly! That was when he said the money had come originally from people who had no more right to it than he did — and he had pulled it off.'

'Then someone is still lookin' for him.'

That startled her, but after a while she nodded. 'Of course, that has to be it. I was thinking of the law being after him, but it's more likely it's the original owners of the money, isn't it?'

'Maybe not the original. Seems to me he's afraid of the ones he'd stole the money from in the first place.'

'Yes, that makes sense. But I can't help you much, Frank, I have no idea where the money is hidden.'

'You never looked?'

'Of course I did, but without success.' She looked at him steadily. 'Frank, if ever that money is found and taken from Brad, I want it. It's mine — at least I feel I've earned it after all the years of abuse I've had at his hands.'

That made him plenty uncomfortable. 'Well, I guess you've got a point, but I told Logan he and his men could share it with you . . . '

'You had no right! Frank, I really do feel that I've a rightful claim to that money!'

He nodded. 'But to get it, we'll need Logan's help. He's not going to do the job for wages, Angela. He'll want a big share.'

'And half of a hundred thousand dollars is a *damn* big share!'

'You'd have your half, too,' he pointed out quietly.

Her bosom heaved with her breathing and her eyes were narrowed. Their gazes locked and held. Then she took in a long, deep breath. 'All right. I didn't realize I could feel such . . . greed!' She flushed. 'But, you, Frank, how much do you get out of it?'

He shrugged. 'Don't really care.'

'You keep saying that! That money

means nothing to you — no man can refuse fifty thousand dollars!'

'It wouldn't be that much for a start. But — ' He hesitated briefly. 'I've seen how money can tear a family apart, people who professed to love each other, then when cold, hard cash reared its ugly head for divvying-up, they fought each other tooth and nail, screamed themselves into hysteria, drove one to blow out his brains — or whatever he used for brains . . . '

In the silence that followed she asked very quietly, 'Your family, Frank?'

Those wild grey eyes regarded her coldly and then softened a little as he nodded. 'It was my grandfather's will that caused it. Later, I found out he'd swindled people out of their land and that was the basis of his fortune — I rode out in disgust and have never been back.'

'But that was people behaving badly!'

'Money caused it. Since then, I've worked for what I need and gotten by tolerably well, well enough for my wants, anyway. I don't trust easy money, or dishonest money — sure not tainted money. No, I don't want any share of Brad McLane's loot, if it exists. You and Logan can have it all.'

They had left it at that and now the thought of the money had brought him out of bed to sit on a log near the communal camp-fire where he smoked a cigarette.

There had to be some way to take that money away from Brad McLane. Once he had lost it, he would have lost his security, his one hope of escape from whatever enemies were lurking in his background. He would be shaken to the core, terrified — and that was just the way Frank wanted him, totally helpless, reduced to abject fear, jumping at shadows.

'Something troubles you, brother?'

Bryant started at the sound of Doc Hubbard's voice, spun around on the log to see the old sect leader standing there in his pale buckskin robe, packing a pipe. Doc grunted as he sat down on

132

the log beside Frank.

'I think I can handle it, Doc.'

'Star overheard Angela telling you about this man McLane and his hidden riches.'

The words tensed Frank instantly. 'Overheard? You mean she was snoopin'! There was no one else around we could see when Angela told me, so Star had to be in the bushes.'

Hubbard smiled. 'I like to keep my finger on the pulse of happenings in my camp, Frank — don't be offended.'

Bryant shrugged, relaxing slightly. 'Well, I guess it can't do any harm, but I wouldn't like Logan or Nudge to get word on how much it is just yet. Maybe later . . .'

'Perhaps you have a point. Did I ever tell you I come from Canada? No? It's true. I haven't always been leader of our tribe, you know. Once I went the way of most men on the frontiers, the wild way. I boozed and wenched and fought, even robbed before I learned to love our Giver Of Life.'

'Hard to imagine, Doc. Seein' you now.'

'Nonetheless it's true. I ran with a lawless bunch in the back alleys of the ancient city of Montreal. We preyed on the riverboats that steamed the St Lawrence River. There were huge, crooked gambling syndicates, run by French gangsters who had come to the Province of Quebec to escape the law in their own country — it was an evil land at that time. Then suddenly, everything stopped. The gangs collapsed, traitors sought out the police and informed on their leaders. Why? Because the money that ran the gangs had dried up. Gone.'

Bryant was all ears now, remembering that Angela had said McLane's real name was Roberto Rivelle — *French spelling, so I am told*', she had said. 'The backing money was stolen?' he asked.

'By several armed men. They stole the funds that propped up that evil empire and it collapsed. During the chaos, the thieves managed to escape.'

'With a hundred thousand dollars?'

Doc smiled, re-lit his pipe which had gone out. 'More than that. Closer to *two* hundred thousand . . . '

'Judas priest!'

'An immensely rich syndicate of criminals, destroyed by the greed of some of its own members . . . I heard names: one was Bobby Revell, an assassin who had a Spanish mother and French father. His real name, of course, was Roberto Rivelle.'

'Otherwise known as Brad McLane.'

Doc tapped out his pipe. 'I would appreciate you not mentioning any of what I've told you, Frank. My followers know, of course, but — '

'Not Logan or his crew. It's safe with me, Doc. I'm obliged. Now all I've gotta do is figure out a way of takin' that money off Brad McLane.'

8

The Start

The nighthawks were used to quiet duty and didn't figure on this night being any different.

They were wrong.

For a start, the rain had returned, not heavily but in a steady downpour that rattled against their slickers and ran in cold trickles down their necks and into the tops of their halfboots. Still, the cattle were settled down in Far Canyon and the riders could afford to take shelter under overhangs of rock or the spreading branches of elms. Such places were dry enough for them to enjoy a cigarette and even a doze in the saddle.

From time to time, one of them would venture out into the rain and circle the herd in a cursory check.

There were four nighthawks in all, for this was a big herd that had been rounded-up ready for the burning of *B Bar M* into their unbranded hides.

It was a redhaired man named Ginger who took his turn at riding a check — and didn't come back.

Billy-Joe, the halfbreed kid from Nuevo Laredo, got worried and heeled his mount out of the shelter of his overhang, riding across to where Mort Andersen dozed in the saddle, a cold cigarette hanging from his lower lip.

Mort didn't appreciate Billy-Joe waking him. 'Ginger ain't come back,' the kid blurted.

'Judas, so what? He's likely takin' a leak or somethin', maybe found a cave and is snorin' his head off. Damn you, kid, I was just enjoyin' a dream about Hannah, that whore at the Dovecote, the one with the buck teeth . . . '

'I know her. Still got her teeth marks on me. But there ain't no caves Ginger could go into, Mort. You know that.'

'Christ! I dunno where he is and I

don't blame well care. Go ask Larry, if he's awake, an' not dreamin' of whores!'

'I think I better go take a look.'

'Too bad you din' think about that before wakin' me. Go see if he's talkin' with Larry . . . he's under the live oak yonder.'

Billy-Joe wheeled his mount and had ridden only a few paces when the first shot crashed through the night.

'Ah, *Dios*! I knowed somethin' was wrong!' the halfbreed kid said, fumbling to get the folds of his slicker out of the way so he could reach his gun.

By that time there had been four or five more shots and he even saw a dagger of muzzle flame stabbing into the air, over there at the *sealed* end of the canyon.

In moments, the herd had heaved to its feet and with the thunder of a shotgun loosing its charge into the night, they were running.

The bawling sent a thrill of fear through Billy-Joe, prickling his skin, for he had seen a stampede once before and was, in fact, one of the only two survivors. He made a whining sound and forgot about grabbing for his gun, spurred his horse away towards a pile of large boulders against the canyon wall. He had picked out this place a long time ago as a good place to run to if ever there was a stampede. He slammed his mount in between the boulders, hauled rein behind the largest rock and sat hunched in the saddle, watching wide-eyed as four or five riders came thundering out of the night, driving the herd towards the canyon mouth.

Billy-Joe heard a scream, turned quickly and saw Mort go down under the pounding feet of the wild-eyed, horn-tossing steers as they bawled and snorted and ran for the only way out.

It jammed up in no time and the steers piled-up in a bloody heap, wailing, slobbering, groaning, a cacophony that came straight out of Hell.

Ginger was nowhere in sight and

Larry started shooting at the dark riders, but that shotgun roared again and Larry was hurled out of the saddle and soon pounded into the muddy ground by the steers ploughing their way through and over the downed beasts half-blocking the exit. The steers trod on writhing cows underfoot heedlessly, only wanting out of there, away from the thundering guns and shouting riders.

Billy-Joe was shivering now, one wet hand clutching a sixgun. Not that he had any intention of using it, but it gave him a little comfort as he watched wide-eyed and open-mouthed as the riders hazed the last of the steers out over what had become a slaughter-house in the exit.

One of the riders said, 'There was four nighthawks, wasn't there?'

'Other one's hidin' somewhere,' replied a second voice, the words muffled some by the bandanna he had tied over his nose and mouth. 'Leave him be — he can carry the word back to McLane.'

'Rather he was dead!'

'No. We want McLane to know it's started! Let's go!'

How did they find a way through the back into the canyon? wondered Billy-Joe as he watched them ride out after the stampeding cattle. He heard the gunfire as they drove the herd in the direction they wanted, waited a good half-hour, and then eased his mount towards the entrance.

He was almost sick, smelling the blood and body gases and dung from the trampled cattle and his horse snorted and fought the bit. He kicked it around and, holding his breath, looked about him as he cocked his gun.

It seemed all clear and, taking a chance, he jammed in the spurs and made the long night run back towards ranch headquarters. The rain was heavier now and he knew he likely wouldn't make it before the first signs of daylight.

God knows what would've happened to the rest of the cattle by then . . .

There was the faintest of grey streaks in the east now, only a few stars studding the paling sky. The moon had set long since, but there was enough light to see the scattered cattle.

Except for a small tight bunch of a half-dozen steers held by a couple of Logan's men, the rest of the herd that had survived the stampede in the canyon were still running right on to the edge of the *Llano Estacado*, the awesome Staked Plains, treeless, full of hidden buffalo hollows where cunning, freedom-hungry mavericks such as these could hide within spitting distance of a searching army.

It would take McLane's crew many days, possibly weeks, to locate the survivors and round them up again for branding.

'We could've sold 'em,' growled Ned Nudge, tugging down his stained bandanna now and spitting. 'Logan and me know a coupla fellers'd take 'em, no questions asked.'

Frank Bryant wiped sweat out of his

eyes with the kerchief that had, until a few minutes ago, masked his lower face, and shook his head.

'Ned, for a start they're mavericks, not yet broke to the herd mentality. Be hell drivin' 'em in open country. They'd all want to go every which-way; for another thing, you might make a few bucks to burn a hole in your pocket, but that ain't the point of the exercise.'

Nudge glared at Logan who was rolling a cigarette. 'Aim is to take McLane's herds, ain't it? Strip him down. Why not make a few bucks while we do it?'

Logan jerked his head towards Bryant. 'Ask him.'

'Hell with him — you're the boss.'

'Used to be!'

Bryant shook his head slowly, detecting the hostility in Logan now. 'Look, I'm not tryin' to take over anythin'. You said you wanted to be in this, and I've got it started now, got the plan runnin' around inside my head. Just trust me for a spell and you'll come out of this richer than you ever dreamed.'

'How you expect us to b'lieve that when you're throwin' good money away?' snapped Ned. 'Like half the hundred thousand to that woman!'

Frank sighed. 'Ned, she's more right to the money than any of us. Logan, you've got enough brains to figure things out. See if you can convince this fool.'

'Now wait a minute!' Nudge dropped a hand to his gun butt.

Bryant set his gaze on him. 'Well? You gonna draw or not?'

'Hold up!' snapped Logan, before Ned Nudge could do or say anything. 'Just calm down, Ned. All I know is we let Frank have his head for a bit and we've got a chance at a slice of that hundred grand of McLane's. Sure, we might miss a handful of dollars by not rustlin' the Bar M steers, but it's peanuts to what's waitin' . . . '

'But we gotta *trust* him, Logan! An' I dunno as I do trust him.'

'Let's see what happens,' Logan said,

and Ned took some more convincing before reluctantly he snarled agreement.

'But you an' me're gonna go head on sooner or later, Bryant!'

'Make it later, Ned. I've got no urge to kill you just now.'

Logan had to settle things down again and then they began driving the half-dozen steers they had kept — for meat for the camp — towards the distant hills. The heavy rain would wash out their tracks, just as it would wash out the churned-up trail left by the stampede.

Brad McLane was going to have one hell of a time even finding his cattle and then he would have the long round-up all over again.

'We should've nailed that fourth nighthawk,' Ned muttered, wanting the last word. 'He makes it back to the ranch fast we could see a bunch of riders comin' outa them hills before we make it to our own trails.'

'Don't think he'd ride too fast.

McLane don't like gettin' bad news,'
Logan allowed. 'He's the kind who's
likely to kill the messenger . . . '

★   ★   ★

McLane came close to doing just that
when the nervous Billy-Joe brought him
the news about the stampede of the
maverick herd.

'Who the hell was it?' the rancher
demanded, raging.

'Dunno, boss. They was masked.'

McLane frowned at the sodden,
muddy, frightened kid. 'How come they
let you live?'

Billy-Joe swallowed. 'One said, 'We
want McLane to know it's started'.'

'*What*'s started, for hell's sakes! What
the Sam Hill does that kind of remark
mean?'

He turned to the cadaverous man in
dark-brown corduroy trousers and
matching vest over a pale-brown shirt.
This was the man they called the
Widowmaker, real name Carey Budd, a

born killer who seldom spoke or offered an opinion unless he was trying to provoke someone.

'What you reckon, Carey?'

'Might be you'll lose more cows,' the Widowmaker offered succinctly.

McLane was silent briefly, then swore savagely. 'Yeah — it's likely that goddamn Bryant! 'Cause I wouldn't pay the ransom! So he figures to take it out in my cows! Like *hell*! Kid, you see where they drove the cows?'

'Wasn't no way to drive 'em, boss. They was a'runnin' and din' look like they'd stop this side of Doomsday.'

'Mightn't be rustlin',' allowed Carey Budd quietly, and they looked at him, awaiting further information.

'Then what the hell *might* it be?' demanded McLane, pushing for an explanation.

'Mebbe tryin' to scare you. Change your mind about the ransom.'

'Aah, you're loco.' McLane hadn't meant to use that word, saw the stiffening of Budd's shoulders and added quickly, 'I mean, *he*'s loco if he thinks that'll make me cough up twenty grand for that bitch! Like I told him, he can have her, chop her up if he wants, feed the coyotes. I won't lift a finger to help her.'

'One other possibility.'

McLane snapped his head around to the gunslinger.

'What?'

'Our old friends.'

The rancher took his time trying to figure out what the man meant and his face paled some, but then he shook his head.

'No! I'm clear. They haven't picked up on me all this time. No reason why they should now.'

'There's one.' As McLane's eyes widened, the Widowmaker said, 'If they been watchin' me. Don't think they have, but if they were and you've hired me..' He shrugged his bony shoulders. 'They know we always got along.'

McLane sat down heavily and didn't seem to hear when Billy-Joe asked if it was OK for him to go get a cup of coffee from the cookhouse as he was frozen to the bone after the ride through all that rain.

When it became clear the rancher wasn't going to answer, maybe hadn't even *heard*, Carey Budd jerked his head at the door.

'Go get your java, kid. Tell the crew they better get ready to go look for them mavericks.'

Billy-Joe cleared out quickly. He was always glad to get out of sight of the Widowmaker. The man made his bowels quake, even worse than Fletch Kirby had.

But Kirby was all through now, out of it, gone to kinfolk in Colorado, so it was said — after being cold-bloodedly fired by McLane, and left to find and pay his own way back to limited recovery from his shocking injuries. Off the payroll, out of mind . . . McLane had washed his hands of the man who had served him well for years.

Billy-Joe was giving serious thought

to just riding out and keeping on riding: working for B Bar M was becoming too much of a strain.

And it sounded like things were only going to get worse.

A hell of a lot worse.

9

Rattled

Logan and Ned Nudge came to see Bryant in the camp as a deputation. He had been expecting it all week but he showed nothing as they came up to where he was mending a cinch-strap in the sun outside his cabin. Steve Macklin was now walking around without aids and thinking about trying to ride again, leaning on the corral rail, picking out a mount.

'Howdy, boys — take a pew.' Bryant gestured to the log near the camp-fire site and where most visitors sat. He was sitting on a stump-chair, the wooden clamp base under his thighs, the curved jaw holding the strap as he worked with twin needles and waxed thread. He used his teeth to give each thread a final tug before picking up the needle awl and punching in the next holes. He glanced up casually. 'Somethin' on your mind?'

Logan and Ned sat down, their faces sober and hard. 'Yeah! We have that! And I'm here to tell you — '

'Ned!' Logan snapped the word and frowned and scowled, as reluctantly he broke off his tirade.

Bryant stopped sewing the leather and stared at Logan. 'Got a bee in your ear?'

'Got one somewhere. Frank, it's over a week since we hit them mavericks in Far Canyon. The boys I sent to watch B Bar M say they've managed to round-up maybe five hundred head. That's damn good goin', way better'n we figured. In another week he'll have 'em all.'

'No he won't.'

'Why won't he?' snapped Ned, butting in and ignoring Logan's warning look. 'Pinto says looks like they're gonna drive that five hundred back and start brandin', or mebbe they'll do it right where they're holdin' 'em now! I knew that damn raid'd come to nothin'!'

'Finished?' Frank asked, mildly, and his gaze took in both men. 'The purpose of that raid was to stir things up.'

'So you reckon!' Ned snapped, refusing to stay quiet.

'Well, McLane's been stirred,' Bryant continued mildly, as if Ned hadn't spoken. 'He's had to call in his men from other parts of the ranges and right now, accordin' to Logan's boys, he's got most of B Bar M's crew on the edge of the Llano. And they'll stay there if he starts the brandin'.'

'Which'll put him back on schedule, or nearly so!'

'Yeah — he'll be startin' to relax, think that was just a one-off raid to let him know we weren't happy about him not payin' the ransom.'

'Well, you can say that again, brother!' Ned was bitter. 'Just between you an' me, I still ain't happy about it!'

'Ransom's not an issue now, Ned, we're tryin' to get our hands on the hundred grand,' growled Logan. 'Forget the piss-ant ransom, will you?'

Ned glared but remained silent.

'The thing is,' continued Frank, 'he thinks things are settlin' down. So we let him think that. Then, when he's ready to brand, or drive 'em back to some other holdin' place on B Bar M, we hit him again, send 'em to hell-an'-gone — and he's got to start all over again. *And*, with a little luck, we'll even have a surprise waitin' for him when he gets back to his ranch.'

Both outlaws frowned but, of course, it was Ned who growled, 'And what the hell is all that gonna gain us? We gonna go round in circles, hittin' an' runnin'?' He shook his head savagely. 'No damn point in it! Don't get us any nearer that *dinero*!'

'You're wrong, Ned. Every time we hit him and it seems pointless, us not tryin' to rustle his stock or so on, it's gonna get McLane all worried and confused.'

'Judas priest!'

Bryant held up a hand irritably. 'Why don't you shut down and *listen* for a change, Ned?'

That brought Ned off the log, charging in with fists cocked, easily thrusting Logan aside as he tried to stop him. Frank whipped the wooden saddleclamp from under his thighs and, as Ned swung, came up inside the arm and beat the man on the head with the heavy wooden base. Ned staggered, shaking his head, one leg buckling. He swung backhanded and Frank dodged, hit him again with the clamp, driving him to his knees.

Ned twisted and clumsily punched at Frank's midriff. It connected and stopped Bryant for a moment but he sucked down a breath and, as Ned came surging to his feet, swinging, clubbed him once more, and again, and swung a final blow that dropped Ned against the log, one arm draped limply over it, his face streaked with blood.

'You buyin' in?' Bryant asked Logan, who looked as if he might do just that but the young outlaw shook his head. 'Reckon not.'

'Good!' Frank dropped the clamp and straddled Ned's dazed figure, twisting fingers in the man's hair, wrenching his head back so he was looking up at Frank with pain-filled eyes.

'Time to end this, Ned. You can either listen, or get up and go for your gun — which'll it be?'

Ned blinked blood out of his eyes, tried to scowl but ended up just nodding.

'What's that mean?' prodded Frank.

'No . . . gun.'

'Fine. Now listen. McLane's hidin' that money somewhere on B Bar M. We don't know where and far as I'm aware, neither does anyone else — only McLane. Now we could jump him and use Injun torture and sooner or later he might break. *Might*, I say, because he's just mean enough to die on us so he won't have to tell us.'

'So — what d'we do?' Ned slurred, spitting some blood. 'Stampedin' his cows won't make him tell us.'

Frank glanced at Logan and shook his head. 'Ned, stampedin' his herds and whatever else we do, isn't planned to make him *talk*, for Chris'sakes! It's to shake the bejeebers outa him, scare him white — and what you think he'll do if he's scared witless, Ned?'

Even then Ned Nudge had to think about it and Logan, exasperated, said, 'Judas, Ned, use your goddamn brains. *He'll begin to think the ones he stole the money from are comin' after him!* That that's why his herds aren't bein' rustled, only harassed, each time worse than the other. So . . . you got it figured yet?'

Ned blinked. 'He'll . . . grab the money and . . . run?'

Logan spread his hands, half-smiling at Frank. 'By hell, I think he's got it, Frank!'

'Well, what blamed good does that do us? He snatches his *dinero* and runs with it . . . Oh!' The penny dropped for Ned at long last. 'Aw, now I get it — we move in before he runs.'

'But after he digs his money outa wherever he's got it cached,' Frank said quietly. 'That's it, Ned. We hassle the hell outa him until he figures he better grab his money and run while he still can. We watch and we wait and when he's ready to ride for the Border, we move in.'

'You heard of the Widowmaker?' Logan asked quietly.

Bryant nodded slightly. 'Sure. Name's Carey Budd — half loco, they say. Gets some kinda sex thrill from killin' folk.'

'He's McLane's bodyguard you know.'

'I know.'

'It don't bother you?'

'I've never seen him in action — I won't know till we square-off.'

'Christ, man! You'd call him?'

'If that's what it takes.'

'Rather you than me!'

'That's OK — I'm willin' to take the chance. If I have to face Budd so I can get to McLane, I'll do it. I'd face Satan himself.'

'Well, if the gal knows what she's talkin' about, and Doc Hubbard, McLane won't be any push-over, neither.' This observation was from Ned and there was almost pleasure in it at the thought there might be a chance of Bryant being killed — and as long as it didn't stop them getting their hands on the money, why the hell not?

It'd be no skin off Ned's nose.

★ ★ ★

Almost every rider belonging to B Bar M had been recruited to round-up and bring in the mavericks scattered all over the southern part of the Staked Plains.

'I want 'em branded and ready for the trail by the nineteenth,' McLane told the men. The man who had replaced Fletch Kirby as ramrod was named Wes Pardoe, a trail-tough veteran who had always felt out of place on B Bar M, but simply couldn't pass up the good money that McLane paid for his expertise.

It had riled the hell out of Pardoe to take orders from someone like Kirby and he wasn't in the least sorry the man had been crippled by this Bryant — who was obviously a much tougher nut than McLane gave him credit for. Now he was officially ramrod and could give the orders, he used his vast knowledge of cattle and round-ups and trail drives to the full. The ranch had never operated more efficiently.

On the quiet, McLane was realizing he had been under-using the old streak of misery all this time.

'Main herd won't be ready by the nineteenth, boss,' Wes Pardoe told McLane, hawking and spitting phlegm. He had an annoying cough that many of the cowpokes complained kept them awake nights.

'Did I say anything about the main herd?' snapped McLane. 'I said I want them mavericks branded by that time. I know they're ready for the trail, we can soon round-up the other critters that are used to it. Make good savvy?'

Pardoe had to admit it did. 'I'll put another four men on to it.'

'Four? Put every man on the payroll out there.'

'Too many, and they'll be fallin' over each other — four's more'n plenty.'

McLane glared. 'You lookin' to buck me, old man?'

'You're payin' me top wages, Mr McLane; I'm just tryin' to give you your money's worth.'

McLane grunted. 'Do what you like then — just have 'em ready by the nineteenth.'

Wes rode away, hawking again, and McLane sat craggy-faced on his buckskin with the white mane and took a cigar out of his pocket. He bit off the end, spat it out, took a match and snapped it into flame on his thumbnail. Through the cloud of smoke he puffed, he saw Pardoe had men gathering the cows which had already been rounded-up, readying them for the short drive down to Cat Tail Canyon where men were already preparing the branding fires and holding pens.

Yeah, the oldster knew his ranch work, all right. Push him just a little and he might regain some of the time lost by that Queer raid ten days ago . . .

By afternoon the herd was being driven down to Cat Tail. It was a tough job, riding through choking dust, the still half-wild animals breaking away constantly.

But by round about four o'clock they had started to behave better, were staying bunched up for longer periods. This way they would be down at Cat Tail before sundown. McLane reckoned he could bully old Wes into making the men start the branding, working by firelight, just to get the job done quickly.

Of course, he would offer to pay extra — but just how much extra he would decide come pay-day. And it mightn't be what the men were expecting but — so what! By then the work would've been done. What could they do? *Unbrand* the cows?

He chuckled at the thought and dropped even further back behind the bustling, cursing, riding cowboys as the herd moved on down trail. Yeah, it was all going to work out OK and he could thumb his nose at this Bryant. The man must already realize he had wasted his efforts on stampeding the maverick herd.

And he surely must know by now McLane was never going to pay any ransom for that bitch of a wife of his . . . McLane hauled rein sharply, feeling the shock drain the blood from his face and clench his heart as the sudden gunfire blasted through the afternoon dust haze. It came from the slopes of the hills either side of the wide trail that led back to Cat Tail Canyon on B Bar M land.

Brad McLane fought the prancing buckskin and his eyes widened in disbelief as he saw half-a-dozen mavericks fall.

They were killing his cattle!

'No!' he yelled, and spurred forward, lashing at the buckskin with his quirt, seeing Pardoe's riders spinning in circles, trying to find where the shooting was coming from.

There was another ragged volley and two cowboys fell out of their saddles this time, as four more cows crashed to the dust where they kicked and bawled, wounded or dying — and scaring hell out of the rest of the spooky herd.

The rancher was still riding in when suddenly the herd shattered, broke in every direction imaginable, cowboys hauling their mounts quickly out of the way of raking horns as fear and panic took over.

'Not again!' wailed McLane to himself, spurring the buckskin up a rise to haul rein in amongst some boulders where he was safe from both the now stampeding herd and bullets from the attackers.

The cows whirled and veered and weaved and somehow formed up into a wedge that raised ten times more dust than before, the hills echoing to the bawling thunder of all-out stampede. One cowboy at least didn't make it out of the way, went down screaming, his horse thrashing, half-rising from out of the midst of the charging herd, his hide torn and bloody, before falling back. His carcass brought down several steers and there was a pile up briefly before those pushing from behind made a way around the bloody mess.

Guns were still crashing and McLane, fuming but afraid of being hit, crouched down amongst the rocks and watched and listened to the last ten days' mighty hard work being destroyed . . .

Just when he figured everything was going to be fine.

★   ★   ★

By nightfall it was clear that they weren't going to get any more of the

165

cattle back. They had managed to corner about thirty and were still having trouble holding them in hastily made rope-and-brush corrals.

McLane knew they would likely make a rush and break out during the night — they were still within earshot of the rest of the herd scattered all over the goddamn Staked Plains again, bawling to each other . . .

'Forget it, Wes,' McLane called hoarsely. 'Forget it, man. We'll have to start over again come sun-up. And I want every damn ranny that works for me out here, working those cows!'

'Don't think we're gonna make your deadline, boss,' Pardoe said quietly, weariness making his voice quaver.

'Do what you can,' Brad McLane said. 'Me and Carey are going back to the ranch. You do your best — and it better be good enough.'

Always had to have that last barb twistin' in a man's hide, Wes thought, as the rancher rode off with that damn morbid shadow at his side, just looking for a chance to put a bullet in someone — *anyone*, from what the men said.

McLane was mighty tired by the time they reached the dark ranch yard. He told the Widowmaker to roust the cook and tell him he wanted supper in twenty minutes — and it had better be a full and proper meal. Not long after Angela's kidnapping — if that's what it was — he had fired the Mexican woman cook, but had to admit he hadn't eaten as well since that time.

Anyway, he would eat well this night or the present cook would have his ass kicked clear off B Bar M. In fact, he was in such a lousy mood, he might even turn Carey Budd loose on the man . . .

Someone had to pay for that upset with the herd! By God, if that Bryant was behind it — he stopped. Who the hell else could it be? Those men up in Canada?

He felt the coldness snake through his body at the thought but shook his head quickly.

No — it couldn't be. It was Bryant, all right, and, by hell he was going to pay —

Suddenly the barn exploded.

Brad McLane was looking right at it, saw a flare of some kind briefly light up the inside of the barn, and the next instant it was reduced to splintered timbers, whirling and buzzing as they flew around the ranch yard, windows cracking like pistol shots in the house, roof shingles pattering down into the yard like rain — two of them hitting McLane on the shoulder, drawing a startled and painful yell from him, and driving him to his knees.

Then he spread out on his face and covered his head with his arms as the roaring explosions tore at his ears and flame and gouting dirt and debris filled the night.

10

Ride 'Em Down!

Carey Budd charged out of the house, gun in hand, saw the flaming remains of the barn and stepped back hurriedly on to the porch as shingles and bits of debris rained down.

He glanced across the yard, saw the dazed McLane stagger to his feet and started towards the rancher, then stopped abruptly. The flames were big enough and bright enough to light up some of the land around the barn, the yard in front — and behind.

The Widowmaker brought up his gun and fired two fast shots at a moving shadow back there running towards the line of trees. He climbed up on to the porch rail, triggered again, then jumped down into the yard and sprinted for his mount which was still saddled down by the corrals.

Brad McLane, dirty and dishevelled, massaging his hurt shoulder, blinked as the gunman ran past.

'OK?' snapped Budd, without pausing.

'I guess. What the hell you shooting at?'

'Someone back there — runnin' for the trees.'

The words brought McLane more alert and he looked around but could see nothing beyond the burning remains of the barn. But sudden anger raged through him. Even as the Widowmaker hit the saddle in a hurry and wrenched his mount around, he yelled, 'Get after him! Ride him down! Bring the bastard back alive!'

Budd was already thundering out of the yard, swinging wide around the fire, heading for the trees.

The cook was coming towards McLane now, holding out a glass of whiskey, and the rancher took it, drained it at a gulp. 'Get me the goddamn bottle!' he snapped, by way of thanks, his voice shaky as reaction set in.

He weaved his way slowly towards the house as the cook ran back to do as he was told.

McLane was mounting the steps, the roar of the fire filling his head, knowing that there was no point in trying to save what was left of the barn, when a chunk of the awning post beside him ripped loose. He staggered as splinters tore into the side of his face.

The shock more than hurt dropped him to his knees, one shaking hand grabbing at his bleeding face. *Hell, he hadn't even heard the shot!*

But he heard the second one — and the third. The bullets tore chunks of wood out of the rail and a fourth one screeched and whined off the flagged area in front of the big main door, thudding deep into the carved cedar.

Frightened out of his wits now, McLane stretched out on the floor and started yelling for someone to get the door open and help him inside. Three more shots had ripped up the carved horse and longhorns on the door before it swung open a few inches and McLane hurled himself against it, rolling into the passage, yelling, 'Close it! Close it!'

The cook's eyes were bulging and his own hands were shaking as he handed the rancher a bottle of whiskey. McLane took it and sloshed a good deal down the front of his crumpled, dirty shirt before getting some in his mouth. He had to hold the bottle with both hands and the neck rattled against his teeth.

'What we gonna do, boss?' asked the frightened cook.

McLane merely stared at him, wide-eyed, then took another deep swig from the bottle.

Two windows in the house's top floor shattered and falling glass shards tinkled on the porch awning. McLane huddled in close against the wall, hearing the flat, dull sounds of the gunfire, muffled by the heavy doors and log walls.

The bullets couldn't reach him in here, of course, unless he was stupid enough to poke his head up above the window sill . . .

Then he froze.

There was a single shot followed by a sound in the yard that chilled his blood.

A horse whinnying in terror and pain.

'Oh, God, no!' he breathed, recognizing the sound of his buckskin with the white mane.

He had left it standing with trailing reins down by the corrals.

He risked taking a quick peek out of one of the parlour windows. The horse was still there — but down on the ground now, thrashing in its death throes.

* * *

Within the line of trees beyond the burning barn, Frank Bryant paused to look back as he heard the gunfire raking the yard and the ranch house.

He could see two men in the yard, one running fast for the porch steps, the other staggering on behind. That one would be McLane and he grinned tightly — the man was obviously groggy. He was lucky he had been caught only on the edge of the explosion.

Bryant had timed it that way, lighting the fuses to the bundles of dynamite he had planted while McLane and his crew were out rounding-up the mavericks, with only a few house staff left at the ranch. Fixing the explosives in the barn was no problem: in fact, he had had a light sleep in the hayrick while awaiting McLane's return.

When he had seen McLane and the Widowmaker riding in, he had started to light his fuses and then made his run, not for the trees, because he knew he would never make it before the barn blew. But he had picked out a depression in the ground almost halfway to the treeline and he dropped flat in the bottom of this just as the barn exploded.

It had been a complete success and, his ears ringing with the sound of the blast, he had started for the trees and his mount.

Now he heard the gunfire, turned in time to see the porch raked by bullets, McLane down and rolling towards the heavy front door. As the door opened wide enough to let the panicked rancher hurl himself inside, Frank saw Carey Budd riding hell-for-leather towards him, gun coming up.

The man put a couple of bullets close to Bryant as he weaved into the trees and found his ground-hitched mount waiting with pricked-up ears and tensed muscles. Budd had paused to slide his empty six-gun back into his holster and whip out his rifle from the saddle. Bryant hit the stirrup at a run, flung his other leg over and, at the same time, slapped the reins free of the rock that was holding the ends to the ground.

He had the reins in his hands and the

horse turned before Budd got off his first rifle shot. It rattled high amongst the branches, bringing down leaves and twigs, and Frank drew his Colt and punched three fast shots behind. He glimpsed Budd swerving aside and then, as Frank turned front, ready to concentrate on getting away, lying low on the horse, using his spurs sparingly and allowing the animal to weave its own way through the trees, he saw Budd wheel hard left and make off in that direction.

Puzzled, briefly, Frank then realized the man had also heard the gunfire raking the house, and maybe had spotted the muzzle flashes, and was now riding after the shooter.

He slowed, started to turn back, and heard a thunder of riders closing in, men calling, wanting to know what had happened. He swore. Men riding in an attempt to gather in some of the cattle which had been stampeded along the trail must have heard the explosion and come back to see what was wrong.

There was a crash of gunfire. He saw a man sway in the saddle. Then the riders, and Budd, brought up their guns and pumped lead into rocks on a small rise. He heard the buzzing ricochets and, even at this distance, instinctively hunched lower in the saddle.

'I see the sonuver!' someone yelled, and there was more shooting, a concentrated volley, delivered with spite and hostility, a release after the stampede had caught the cowboys flatfooted and helpless.

Frank saw a man rear up from the rocks, stagger as more bullets tore into him, and then topple forward to crash on his face and skid a couple of yards before coming up short against a tree.

Budd and B Bar M riders rode forward to see who they had shot and Frank Bryant got out of there.

There was nothing he could do to help the rifleman.

Whoever he was.

★ ★ ★

It was full daylight by the time Frank rode into the camp deep in the Trinity Breaks.

The others were there, enjoying after-breakfast coffee and cigarettes. Angela brought him a tin platter of bacon and beans and some fresh bread baked by Star.

'You have blood on your right shoulder,' she said, her eyes checking him over.

Frank was surprised: he hadn't felt a bullet clip him. He had been riding away from the Widowmaker, of course, and the man's shots had been high. Then Angela, cleaning the shallow wound, took out a splinter of greenwood and there were leaves caught in his shirt material. As she worked, she said, 'Seems as if it wasn't a bullet at all. You must've caught it on a broken branch or something.'

'More'n likely. Widowmaker only got off a couple of shots before he turned back.'

'Turned back?' she asked, puzzled.

'That's not like him to give up so easily.'

The others were still winding-down from the success of the raid on the mavericks and before Frank could answer the woman, Logan came across, lighting a cigarette. He squatted down, grinning.

'They'll be chasin' them cows clear across into New Mexico, I reckon. We heard the barn go. Wish I could've seen it.'

'Spectacular,' Bryant told him. 'What the dynamite didn't destroy, the fire would have.'

Logan nodded towards the shoulder. 'Who did that?'

'Ran into a tree — don't see Steve around.'

Logan looked around vaguely. 'Still sleepin', I guess.'

'With the racket you fellers are makin'?'

Frank looked quizzically at Angela and she said, 'Steve rode out during the night.'

Logan frowned as Bryant stiffened. 'Where?'

'He said it was time he did something himself to square with Brad for lashing him across the face with his quirt and allowing Fletch Kirby to almost kill him. We tried to stop him, but he was adamant.'

'So that's who it was,' Frank breathed, and, as they both stared, he said, tight-lipped, 'Someone started shootin' at McLane after the barn blew and he was runnin' for the house. Almost got him a couple of times . . . Damn it!'

'What's wrong with that?' demanded Logan. 'Sounds like a good idea. Scare the pants off him after the stampede and the barn blowin' up. Wish I'd thought of it.'

'You'd be dead if you had.'

Angela drew down a sharp breath. 'Steve was — killed?'

He nodded, told how Budd must have spotted Macklin, rode back just as riders came in from chasing the stampeding mavericks, no doubt attracted by the barn's explosion.

'Tough luck,' Logan opined.

'Tougher than you know,' Bryant said, getting their full attention. 'They'll recognize Steve, of course, and figure he's behind the stampedes and blowing the barn — '

'Well, that's OK, ain't it? Take the pressure off us.'

'No it damn well ain't OK! If McLane figures Macklin was behind it, he'll figure it was Steve's way of gettin' back at him for lashin' him with the quirt, just like Angela said.'

'So what?' Logan was irritated now.

'You still don't get it? Man, if McLane figures it that way and Steve's now dead, he won't be figurin' it was anyone from Canada comin' after him and — '

He paused and Angela nodded slowly. 'And he won't grab his money and make a run for it!'

Frank nodded. 'Yeah — it means we'll have to start all over again.'

★ ★ ★

'I told you to bring him back alive, goddamnit, Carey!'

Brad McLane's rage made no impression at all on the Widowmaker as the rancher looked down at the bullet-riddled body of Steve Macklin lying at the foot of the porch steps.

'The boys didn't know that. One of 'em spotted Macklin's hidy-hole in the rocks and they all opened-up — was too late by the time they stopped firin'. Must've shot half a box of slugs into them rocks.'

McLane sighed and nodded resignedly. Things seemed to be getting beyond his control. Nothing was working out as he had planned lately.

'Anyway, you know who's behind all the trouble now.'

The rancher snapped up his head, looked scathingly at Budd and then down to the torn body of Macklin.

'He wouldn't've had the brains to think up anything like what's been happening around here! He was just a dumb cowpoke who could use a gun tolerably well, but had to have every damn order spelled-out for him.'

'Well he could've teamed-up with this Bryant. I'm pretty sure that's who it was lightin' a shuck for the trees behind the barn. Just as you described him to me, even the clothes.'

McLane gave it some thought, hesitated, lips pursed, then slowly nodded. Inwardly, Carey Budd sneered: bully-boy rancher convincing himself because he didn't want to believe the men from Canada had finally tracked him down.

Mind, the Widowmaker would rather have it that Bryant and Macklin had been behind the troubles that had plagued B Bar M. *He* had no wish to tangle with those Quebec hombres again. As it was, they couldn't even be sure he had been in on the robbery with McLane — or Rivelle, as they knew him — but he had disappeared about the same time as did the money and they knew he had been friendly with McLane. They weren't dumb: it had just been a small slip in security that had allowed Rivelle to see the money was unguarded briefly — and he had struck, without plan, just grabbed it and run, taking Budd and a few other men he trusted with him.

It had cost plenty to get them out of Canada and down across a dozen states, moving from one to the other, laying false trails, killing where they had to, until, finally, it had seemed it was safe to stop and spend some of the loot.

Rivelle had chosen the South, while Budd and the others had taken their share — a hell of a lot smaller than Rivelle's for the man had hogged most of the loot — and gone their ways. By a bit of luck, Carey Budd had tracked Rivelle down just after he himself had run out of *dinero*. And at the right time, for Rivelle, now McLane, had been in need of a personal bodyguard.

And here they were, McLane scared, but recovering now, figuring his next move. The Widowmaker was kind of sorry he had put the notion in the man's head that the cause of his troubles was only Macklin and this Bryant *hombre*. He should've pushed the notion to the rancher that the men from Canada were coming and then he might've run with the money —

But not far: Carey Budd would've seen to that.

Still, there was always a chance he might grab the cash and make his run and he would need Budd to protect him.

He would pay a high fee, of course, but nothing anywhere near the amount of getaway money McLane could lay his hands on.

'So what's it to be, boss?' Carey Budd asked the thoughtful rancher. 'We stayin' — or we makin' our run for the Border?'

McLane snapped up his head. 'The Border? Just because this damn sod-buster and his pards think they can get away with hassling me? Like hell! We not only stay here, we give the sons of bitches the biggest, bloodiest fight since

Custer at the Little Big Horn! I'm gonna have the boys tear the Trinity's apart till I find this Bryant and where he's holed-up!'

The Widowmaker's face gave away nothing of his thoughts. But inwardly he was cursing himself once again for shifting McLane's thoughts away from the avenging men from Quebec.

11

Hunters

Logan, at Bryant's suggestion, sent a couple of his men to watch the B Bar M.

They rode in just before sundown one day and reported what they had seen. Both seemed a little bewildered.

Hog Wilde, actually a quiet, middle-aged rider who spent much of his time carving idols and sun symbols for Doc Hubbard's tribe, said he didn't savvy it at all.

'Only coupla men back at the ranch house, but Jonesy there, says there cain't be, 'cause there's only a few out on the range. Dunno where the rest are.'

'That's right,' spoke up Jonesy, a hard, muscular man with a pleasant face, although it bore quite a few scars around the eyes and mouth from past fist fights. 'Four men holdin' the main herd, but armed to the teeth, every one of 'em with a shotgun, a rifle and two six-guns. The saddle-bags are bulgin' and you can see there's boxes of shells in there by their shape through the leather. Crammed in tight.'

'How about out on the Llano?' asked Bryant quietly. 'They got most of the men hazin' the mavericks?'

Both Hog and Jonesy shook their heads and Wilde said, 'Don't seem to be botherin' about 'em, Frank.'

Bryant and Logan exchanged glances. 'Then where the hell are all McLane's men?' the latter asked, and there was a touch of worry in his question.

'Perhaps I can tell you,' spoke up Doc Hubbard, who had been sitting nearby, apparently communing with the sun god, although it was obvious he hadn't missed a word of what was being said by the other group.

They all watched him expectantly now as he came and joined them, squatting down with a slight grunt, his long buckskin robe falling loosely about his moccasined feet.

'Some of our Indians have — er — a little trouble following our teachings and style of life. Every so often, a few of them slip away to the outskirts of Masthead and trade a few trinkets, or the odd nugget of gold for the white man's demon likker — I have no real objection, except that the foul brew lowers their inhibitions and sometimes the old Indian savagery shows through and they find themselves in trouble with the law. It seems that Man-Of-Storms himself went in yesterday with two or three others and a white man was killed — with an Indian hunting knife that Storm had traded earlier for a jug of likker. Naturally, the sheriff, when he found Man-Of-Storms sleeping off his drunk down at the river's edge, arrested him and threw him in jail.'

'That's natural for this neck of the woods?' asked Bryant.

'Sad to say it is. It's happened before and although the dead man was considered 'white trash' by the folk of Masthead, Storm was charged with his murder — and it was expected he would eventually pay the ultimate price . . . '

'Well, hell, can't you help him?' Frank demanded.

'I have — as much as I could. The sheriff, although favouring Brad McLane, respects me and allowed me to approach the judge, another of McLane's friends, and he reluctantly agreed to release Storm in my custody until the trial in a couple of weeks' time.'

'Well, I hope things work out for Storm, Doc, but how's this explain where McLane's men are?'

Hubbard looked a little uneasy and it startled Frank for he had never seen the man lose even a little composure before.

'This may've been set-up, Frank. While in jail, Man-Of-Storms was approached by McLane, offered money, or all the whiskey he could drink, if he would lead McLane *and his men* to our camp here in the hills. Storm refused, of course — he would never knowingly give away our position.'

Frank sat up straight. '*Knowingly?*'

Doc Hubbard smiled thinly. 'Don't worry, Frank. Storm, hung-over or not, would never betray us. So, after he told me, we laid false trails through the hills that would lead anyone trying to track us away in the opposite direction — and we did glimpse a rather large bunch of horsemen on Smoke Mountain while we were making our way over the high ridge above the Trinity River. That was the direction we had laid our false trail.'

'Judas priest!' breathed Ned Nudge. 'So McLane's outsmarted us! Or tried to. Set-up Storm, told the sheriff and judge to let you take him, then set men to track you to us.'

'Which only goes to show he reckons

it was Steve and me hasslin' him and not the men from Canada.' Frank tightened his mouth, angry. 'All that work for nothin'!'

'Listen, hot-shot,' spoke up Nudge harshly. 'You said we have to start all over again — well, why ain't we? 'Stead of sittin' here talkin' about Injuns.'

The others chorused agreement, looking at Bryant for an answer.

'I wanted to know where McLane had his men first.'

'Well, now you know; so when do we move, and what do we do?'

Nudge was on the prod, a mean man, ornery enough to want to see Frank put down at any price — even at the cost of a share in the big money.

Bryant smiled thinly. 'McLane's lookin' for us, so why don't we go meet him — say, in Lampblack Pass.'

Logan started. 'That knife slash? Hell, we could easily pick 'em off in there but what'd be the point? That won't help us find the loot!'

Ned and the others growled in

support of Logan. Frank held up a hand.

'We don't kill 'em — only those we have to. But we do get us *one man* and bring him here — wait a minute! Bring him here *blindfolded*. I'll explain what we do with him afterwards.' He stood. 'Logan, you'll take your men, except for Curly who'll come with me and help me plant charges of dynamite at both ends of Lampblack Pass.'

'*Both* ends?'

'Yeah — seal it up. They'll get out eventually but that's OK. By that time you and your men will have burned a couple of line shacks, used the last stick of dynamite on the headgates of the Bar M dam and flooded McLane's summer pastures — and raised any other kind of hell you can think of.'

'And . . . ?'

'Let's get that far first, OK? If it works out like I hope, McLane'll grab his money and run — and we'll be waiting.'

They discussed it but liked the idea.

Frank saw Angela standing near his cabin and walked across, leaving the others talking and arguing the pros and cons of his plan.

She studied him soberly. 'Frank, I've been wondering. I'm supposed to get half of Brad's cache of money and Logan and his men get the other half — what do you really get out of this? You say you don't want money, but there has to be *something*.'

His battered face was very sober when he said, 'I see McLane reduced to nothin'. A man like him, wreck his empire, strip him of all his possessions and money, and that's exactly what he becomes — nothin'. And he'll know it. I'll make sure he knows it was me did it — then I'll kill him.'

It was the utter certainty and callousness in his voice more than the words that drained the blood from her face and drove a shudder through her lithe body.

'Frank, I think you're an honourable man. You're doing this for your friend who once saved your life, but will you feel comfortable with it when it's over?'

'It'll satisfy me,' he said, and walked back to where Logan and the others waited.

* * *

It was like a small army.

Brad McLane himself rode in the lead on a muscular black gelding, with the Widowmaker a few feet behind. The main body of men followed, all armed to the teeth but looking weary and, in some cases, even bored.

Among the rocks of the slopes above Lampblack Pass, a name earned because it was so narrow and was in almost perpetual black shadow because of its high walls, Bryant watched through his field-glasses, Curly Bannacek crouched beside him.

'Must be twenty men there,' Frank said quietly.

'McLane only works about thirty,' Curly offered.

Bryant moved the glasses, sweeping back from the main body of riders. 'Someone else comin' through the timber, hundred yards or more back. One man, leadin' three packmules. Guess they're aimin' to stay out lookin' for us until they find us . . . '

Curly took the glasses and looked at the drag rider. 'That's Billy-Joe, just a half-breed Mex-Indio kid. None too bright but they say he can talk to hosses and savvy what they say.'

'He's our man,' Bryant said. 'We get on down there and light our fuses on my signal. Then we drop down and cut off this Billy-Joe, grab him and take him back to camp, blindfolded. And — this is important, Curly — *don't say a word*. Nothing at all. We close in, grab him and that's it.'

Curly clearly wanted to ask why but merely nodded and said, 'What about the mules?'

'Bring 'em along. Doc can always use extra grub.'

'Funny feller, Doc,' Curly said, as

they moved to where they had tethered their mounts. 'Can change the Ten Commandments to suit hisself, and, at the same time, shoot the eye out of a squirrel at a hundred paces. Yet he's always prayin' for somethin' or other . . . man or animal.'

Frank pursed his lips. 'Never knew he could shoot.'

'Aw, yeah — real good. An' I once seen him beat a man to bloody pulp. Some range rider stumbled on the place, got in among the women and deflowered a young gal. Doc went plumb loco. Ended up throwin' the feller in the river, not carin' whether he lived or died. It weren't murder, he said. The man *needed* killin' for what he done.'

Bryant grunted. 'A man with strong convictions is our Doc. And a lot tougher than you'd think.'

They mounted and rode in opposite directions to where their long fuses waited, hidden amongst stones and short grass. Bryant had calculated as well as he could, burning a foot of fuse first and timing it, working out then what length of fuse they would need. He figured it would take McLane and his men about twenty minutes to reach the middle of the pass from where they were now, and cut the fuses accordingly.

If his calculations were correct, both ends would blow, filling the pass with rock and dirt. It may not completely seal the pass but it would delay them long enough for what Frank had in mind.

The riders swung along the trail, old Wes Pardoe out in front now, squatting occasionally to look for sign. 'Don't see no more sign, boss,' he called back. 'But ain't nowhere else for the trail to lead but through the pass.'

McLane looked up at the high narrow walls, studied them carefully. 'Seems OK, but don't lose any time getting through — pass the word down the line.'

He spurred the big black forward,

followed by the Widowmaker who had unsheathed his rifle and kept looking up at the walls. It was a damn good place for an ambush . . . but if they hurried through all should be well.

The men didn't care for the chill shadow that filled Lampblack Pass, either, and spurred their mounts, crowding up into the pass, all eager to be through.

They were just past mid-way when the dynamite blew, the explosion behind them bringing their heads snapping around, setting their hearts thumping. Then, moments later, the second explosion up ahead brought them wrenching back. The air was filled with deafening noise, the sky partly blotted-out by gouts of dirt and hurtling rocks and leaf-stripped bushes.

The horses whinnied, stamping, twisting, looking for a way out of the crowded area. Some riders fell. Mounts panicked, reared, crashed into others. Men crouched blinded by the dust as debris came pelting down on them.

When it cleared, they saw they were trapped. 'Goddamnit!' snarled McLane, filthy, cut above one eye, ears ringing so he could hardly hear himself cuss. 'They got us trapped! But we'll get out! It might take all day, but we'll get out and we'll find the sonuvers — Come on, start moving those rocks . . . *Move*, goddamnit! *Move!*'

Billy-Joe hauled rein fast when he heard the distant explosions, one hard on the heels of the other. He saw the erupting dirt and rocks flung high, fought his frightened mount. The pack mules brayed and rolled their eyes but didn't run, although the hind one kicked out several times at nothing at all.

Billy-Joe heard the rumble of rocks sliding, the muted whinnying of the mounts of the men trapped in the pass. He stood in his stirrups, not sure what he should do.

Then a rope noose dropped over him, pinned his arms halfway down, and he was jerked roughly out of saddle. He hit the ground hard, started to roll, but tension on the rope dragged him back and hauled him part-way up the slope.

His gritty eyes widened as he fought to his knees and saw two riders, both wearing bandannas as masks, coming towards him, one holding the rope. He struggled to get free, was yanked down to his knees again and then on to his back. One rider closed in, leaned from the saddle and clubbed him with a gun butt.

When he regained his senses, Billy-Joe was roped in the saddle, a blindfold, pulled tight, covering his eyes.

'Hey! Where am I? Where you takin' me?'

Someone punched him hard on the shoulder and only the ropes held him in the saddle.

'*Se taire, m'sieur!*' hissed Bryant, hoping he sounded like a Frenchman. Putting on the fake accent that Angela and Doc had tried to teach him, he added, 'Be qui-et! Or *l'mort*! You die!'

Billy-Joe went cold, skin prickling.

He recognized the language, even if he didn't understand it.

For the first time in many years, he began to pray.

★ ★ ★

Several of the men in Hubbard's Tribe Of The Sun came from his native Quebec and spoke French as their native tongue. Star, Lady and a couple of the other women could speak a little and Angela knew some from her schooling.

They kept Billy-Joe blindfolded and tied up in the camp and the only voices he heard were those who could speak French. A little heavily accented broken English was thrown in so that he would be able to report the general gist of things.

He heard the word, *l'mercenaires* several times and once a man said, complaining, 'They call us mercenaries, but where is the mon-ee, eh? *L'argent!* They should pay us now!'

'First the *travail* then *l'argent* — or per'aps *d'or*, eh, *mon ami*! Plenty gold may-bee!'

It was all play-acting, mighty overdone at times, but always within earshot of where Billy-Joe lay, wondering about his fate.

A woman with a soft voice fed him soup and pieces of fresh-baked bread which tasted wonderful to the young 'breed who had eaten indifferent food all his short life.

'Don't worry, *mon ami*,' she whispered. 'They let you go soon.'

'What — what'm I doin' here, ma'am?'

'They want your mules, but did not wish to kill you so bring you here — for now. Soon you go.'

He didn't believe her but later someone shook him, gave him a drink of strong coffee, and he had the impression the man was kneeling in front of him.

'We do not kill young boys,' the unseen man told him in accented

English. 'We let you go later. You know M'sieur McLane?'

'I — I work for him . . . '

'*Bon*. You tell 'im — you say *l'patron*, the boss, he come from Quebec for what ees his. You tell 'im!'

Bill-Joe was shaken again and his face slapped.

'*Comprend? Il est convenu que* — you understand?'

'Judas, yeah! Yeah, I savvy! I tell Mr McLane the boss-man from Quebec is comin' for what's his, right?'

'*Bon! Bon!* Tell 'im, ver-ee soon. *Bientôt!*'

'OK, OK!'

★ ★ ★

Twenty minutes later, Billy-Joe, tied to his saddle again, was led down a darkened trail, still blindfolded. When his mount was stopped he held his breath as a sharp knife slashed the ropes holding him to the saddlehorn. Then his horse was slapped hard on the rump with a hat and it lunged away, snorting, startled into a run immediately.

By the time Billy-Joe had torn off the blindfold and fought the animal to a standstill, he was alone on the slopes near Lampblack Pass.

He rode to the pass itself, saw where the others had moved rocks and earth and dug away so they could lead their mounts up and out of the pass. He climbed up the earthen wall which still stank of dynamite fumes, and called but there was no answer.

They had moved on. It took him an hour before he saw their camp-fires further into the hills and another twenty minutes before he had explained to Brad McLane what had happened.

The rancher's face was drawn and pale when he looked at the Widow-maker. They were standing well away from the main body of men. 'Christ! A bunch of French mercenaries — and they know who I am!'

Carey Budd thought there was

something queer about the whole deal, but he could see where it was leading — drive the frightened McLane to grab his getaway stake and run. The Widowmaker was mighty interested in that money, so he said, 'Been a slip-up somewhere and they've managed to get on to you, boss. Just waitin' for this big shot to come down from Canada. Give him the pleasure of killin' you, mebbe.'

'Jesus, you're a Job's comforter!' snarled the rancher, then sighed. 'But, you're right. That damn Marcel always did like to do his own killing if someone crossed him. We've got to head for the Border, Carey!'

'No use goin' without money, boss,' Budd said slyly. 'You'll need plenty to set yourself up with decent protection down in Mañana Land.'

McLane was nodding jerkily. 'I know, I know — I'm all set for it. You come with me. We'll pick up Carlos at the ranch, leave the boys up here to fight a delaying action. Time they earned the money I been paying 'em . . .'

'They won't like it.'

'They don't have to know. Just tell 'em to keep searchin' for Bryant. If they run into him and his crew . . . ' He shrugged. 'No skin off my nose who survives and who don't.'

'What about the kid?'

McLane glanced across to where Billy-Joe was waiting, fidgeting, nervous, sensing some sort of trouble here. Brad McLane walked across to him, smiling, placed a hand on Billy-Joe's right shoulder.

'You did good, kid. I like a man with spunk. Me and Carey here are going back to the ranch. The others are gonna stay with the search. You come with us. I'd like to give you some kinda reward — after all, you been slugged and tied up and roughed up and you didn't scare. You brought me a message that might just save my life — I appreciate it.'

Billy-Joe smiled awkwardly. 'I — I just done what I had to, boss. I ride for the brand, you know.'

'I know Billy, I know. That's why I don't want to lose you. Now mount up and let's ride. Carey'll give the others their orders and catch up . . . '

The trail McLane and Billy-Joe followed was steep and narrow, high above a deep, brush-choked blind canyon that looked as if it had been resting there since Day Six of The Creation, untouched, brooding — waiting.

Billy-Joe was in the lead, riding slowly, his horse fighting the bit some, not liking the trail. Then, all at once, the kid heard a clatter of hoofs racing up-trail behind him and he flung up an arm, screaming, even as he tried to free a boot from the stirrup.

McLane's spurred claybank smashed into the smaller horse which whickered wildly as it went over the edge, taking Billy-Joe with it, kicking and twisting all the way down.

McLane watched without expression as they hit far below and the thick brush closed over their bodies.

12

Grab The Loot

Logan and Ned Nudge joined Bryant and Curly as they crossed the shallows of Cartridge Creek, once a scene of bloody battle between settlers and a rampaging band of Comanches. So many cartridges had been expended, and the brass casings tossed into the creek later, that a cowpoke mistook it for a carpet of gold. Disappointed, he had named the place, spitting the words with bitterness, and the name had stuck.

Bryant reined in and looked at the two outlaws, right hand on his thigh where he could slide it quickly to gun butt if need be.

'Figured you might need a hand,' Logan said, smiling, but without much warmth. 'Either to take all that *dinero* off of McLane or to lug it back.'

'Reckon we could manage, but seein' as you're here . . . '

Logan's smile widened. 'What I figured — be Johnny-on-the-spot. We seen McLane and the Widowmaker high-tailin' it with that 'breed kid, out towards the river rapids.' His smile had gone now. 'Next time we seen 'em the kid wasn't with 'em.'

Bryant's shoulders tensed. 'What happened to him?'

Logan shrugged and big Ned Nudge said, scowling, 'The hell you think? Don't you know the kinda scum you're dealin' with, Bryant? McLane's lowest of the low.'

'I've had to deal with all kinds, Ned,' Frank told him quietly, looking at the man hard. 'Still am — but weren't no need for McLane to kill that kid.'

'He'd reckon there was. Kid knew who he was from listenin' to us. They're headin' for the ranch now.'

Bryant knew that and now Nudge turned to Curly. 'You ride on back.'

'No, he comes with us.' Ned didn't like it and Logan remained silent as Curly looked from one man to the other. 'Hog said there were four men still at the ranch. We could need an extra gun after all. Specially as McLane seems to be in a killin' mood.'

Frank spurred his mount on, heading off any possibility of argument, and the others followed, Nudge scowling at Curly, who gave him a wide berth.

Bryant rode on ahead, in a killing mood himself.

* * *

Carlos was still at the ranch and, when McLane and the Widowmaker rode in, he stepped out to meet them, rifle in hand.

'Where're the others?' snapped McLane, dishevelled and filthy from the explosion in Lampblack Pass and the ride back.

Carlos whistled and three men stepped out from their hiding places,

211

one by the barn, a second man on the barn roof, and the third by the bunkhouse. At an impatient signal from McLane they came across, guns in hand.

'We're leaving,' the rancher said curtly. 'Bound for Mexico. You boys're the lucky ones. You're coming with us.'

Carey Budd frowned before he could compose his expression: he hadn't figured on a whole bunch heading south. He had thought it would be just himself and McLane.

Not that it made much difference, really; he could handle this bunch with one hand tied behind his back.

'Saddle up the fastest horses and bring spares,' McLane continued, dismounted now. 'I'll get extra ammo from the house and we'll need grub — we won't be going near any towns or well-used trails. There'll be a big bonus for each of you when we get to where I want to go.'

That brought grins to the faces of the hardcases and they ran for the horses.

Carlos moved a little more slowly, looking a shade apprehensively at the Widowmaker. The man still gave him the creeps just by being there. And as long as he was riding along, Carlos knew he would sleep with one eye open — and a hand on a gun butt . . .

Now Carey Budd followed McLane towards the ranch house and suddenly stopped, calling the rancher. When Brad McLane turned, irritably, the gunslinger pointed to the hills.

A smoke column, the base tinged with flame, was rising from the trees on Calico Ridge.

'God-*damn*! My best line camp!' breathed McLane. He looked around a little wildly, as if half-expecting French-Canadian mercenaries to come jumping out of the woodwork.

As, tight-lipped, he turned back towards the house, there came the sound of a dull explosion, far-off, in the north-west. He looked sharply at Budd.

'Oh, my God! The dam!'

'Wasn't much of a bang . . . '

'Christ, it only needs one stick to blow open the headgates ... My pastures are gonna be flooded! My prime beeves will be right in the path of the water!'

'Boss, it don't really matter now,' the Widowmaker told him firmly. 'Let 'em wreck the place. Keep 'em busy while we make our run south — but I reckon we better get a move on.'

'Jesus! All I've worked for, built up over the years ... ' McLane seemed dazed, and then he shook his head, pulling himself together. 'You're right. To hell with the ranch, and to hell with Marcel's hardcases! My hide's all I want to salvage outa this!'

As he flung himself towards the porch steps at a run, Carey Budd said quietly, 'Not quite all, you greedy bastard!'

McLane made Carey Budd wait downstairs and the Widowmaker went into his own room and gathered a few things. Not many to gather at all; he had always travelled light, even in the days up in Canada with McLane — Rivelle, as he was known then — and in permanent work.

He listened but couldn't hear any splintering wood upstairs or the drag of heavy furniture. *Just where the hell had McLane been keeping that money all these years?*

Budd didn't hear the sounds he had been expecting, simply because the money was not hidden in the part of the house used for living.

McLane went to a closet, pushed the clothes aside, and slid back a panel that opened when he pressed a decorative knot in the polished wood. It moved noiselessly and he took out a set of folding wooden steps from a cavity between the walls.

These he set up on the carpet in the middle of his big bedroom, directly under the candelabra that swung there on gilt chains. Two good tugs on one chain and a yank to the left on another freed a panel which swung down silently on a counter-balanced silk rope.

There was a dark, shallow cavity up there that held canvas-sewn packages about six inches deep by a foot square. He took them out one by one, climbing down to drop them on to his big bed, then climbed up one more time and dragged out a folded, dusty leather valise.

A tug on the rope swung the panel back into place and he unbuckled and opened out the valise, and placed the heavy packages inside. He paused with the last one, lowering his head to it, bending it this way and that, hearing the crackle of crisp notes.

He smiled, snatched another valise from the closet after he put away the folding steps, a valise he had kept packed with clothes and shaving gear, a loaded pistol and $1,000 in notes, plus another $200 in gold coins.

He had been ready to flee at a moment's notice for years . . .

Moving quickly and confidently about the big room, he changed into clean clothes and strapped on his sixgun after first checking the loads.

Brad McLane was very much aware that he was carrying a small fortune and that every one of the men who would be riding with him would kill their own mother for a twentieth of what was contained in that valise . . .

They were waiting for him on the porch. He glanced once more at the line camp ridge and noted that the smoke was thinner now — which only meant that the whole camp was well on the way to being reduced to ashes. He looked in the direction of the dam, but it was out of sight, though he could easily visualize the devastation — a roaring wall of water, collecting mud and stones, saplings and bushes on its way, filling the draws and gulches, sweeping away pasture fences, the cattle running in panic, then the muddy water lapping at their heels, climbing relentlessly up their legs, knocking them off their feet. It would be all over in minutes.

Heart slogging in his chest with

barely contained savage anger at what had been done to him, he heaved his valise up to the cantle of the big-chested claybank Carlos had readied for him and tied it on firmly.

Swinging into saddle, eyes hard and raking one last time around the ranch yard and over the house itself, he snapped, 'Let's have no misunderstandings about this, gents, we're going to the Border and anyone tries to stop us, we ride right over the top of 'em. You savvy? No stopping, no deals — let your guns do the talking. Now, let's ride!'

⋆   ⋆   ⋆

Logan led the men in on the high trail overlooking the B Bar M ranch.

They had seen the smoke of the line camp and heard the distant thud of the single stick of dynamite blowing the headgates of McLane's dam.

The plan was working so far — McLane would be already rattled by what Billy-Joe had reported and had wasted no time in getting back to his spread. He and the Widowmaker and four other riders were cutting out across the southern pastures when Logan called a halt on the high trail and pointed.

'Lightin' a shuck! You sure stuck a wild hair up McLane's snoot with that 'French mercenaries' idea, Frank!'

Bryant grunted, busy focusing his field-glasses. He rattled off the names of men he recognized. 'McLane — Carey Budd, Carlos — Mannix and — I think that *hombre*'s called Irish, or Paddy, somethin' like that. Dunno the other one.'

'But there's six of 'em, right?' said Ned Nudge. 'And four of us.'

'Good odds,' Frank said, watching their faces, knowing they were all thinking about the Widowmaker and that the others were McLane's paid guns. 'All we have to do is take the hundred-thousand off 'em, gents.'

Get 'em thinking about the money and they'd take on the whole Apache Nation.

'What's the plan?' asked Logan, taking the glasses and watching the distant riders just as they were disappearing over the edge of a small basin. 'That last man is Dutch Kernahan, by the by, a killer and mean with it.'

'Guess we have to earn our keep,' Frank opined. 'As for the plan — well, the only way we'll get that money is to take it, so let's go do it.'

'Christ! You call that a *plan*?' growled Ned Nudge.

'Sure. You got a better one, Ned?' Frank challenged.

'Well . . . Hell! You mean just ride in a'shootin' an' — '

'What would you do? Tell 'em to put up their hands and then ask 'em to please hand over the money?'

'No, but — '

'Then let's go *take* it, damnit! They're gettin' closer to Mexico with every minute we stay here gossipin'.'

He spurred away and the others followed after an initial hesitation.

'He's right,' Logan said with reluctance. 'There's only one way to do it. Go in shootin'.'

'We're gonna be dodgin' lead!' Nudge complained.

'Like the man said, we earn our money. If you get hit, Ned, you won't have to worry about anythin'. Those sons of bitches will shoot to kill as soon as they see us.'

★　★　★

At Carey Budd's suggestion — and a suggestion from the Widowmaker was as good as any order — the riders bunched up around McLane, surrounding him, offering him protection. That part he liked, the protection, but he was none too easy about being hemmed in by these hardcases.

He knew that they knew he was packing his big getaway stake. There had been rumours flying for years about that and just how much it was. The Widowmaker wouldn't divulge anything, but the others would realise that now McLane was on the run to Mexico he must have it with him. And there wasn't a one he trusted — not even Carey Budd. Not when there was this much money involved.

But there was no choice right now. Anyway, the 'bonus' he had offered need not be too big. A thousand bucks would be *big* bucks to these men. He might even run to two thousand; be generous. That ought to clinch it.

The Widowmaker — well *he* wasn't going to be satisfied with such a pittance, of course. But McLane would worry about that when the situation arose.

'Boss! Boss!'

Carlos's call jarred McLane out of his thoughts. Carlos had ridden on ahead and was now on the trail leading up to a small but high-sided mesa. He came racing down recklessly and reined down hard, standing in the stirrups.

'Bunch of riders comin'! And they're comin' fast!'

'How far back?' snapped Carey Budd.

'Not far enough!'

'Goddamnit! *How far back?*' demanded McLane, in no mood for wisecracks.

'Sorry, boss. Might be a mile.'

McLane went cold. He hadn't expected anyone to be that close. 'Keep riding. And don't bother covering our tracks from here on in. We'll just wait and see who they are. So, unshuck your guns. And if they ain't friendly, shoot to kill — we're not taking prisoners today!'

13

Crossfire

Suddenly, the tracks showed more plainly than they had done previously and Frank was immediately suspicious.

Down on one knee, he examined the trail, turned to look up at the mounted men, Logan, Curly and Ned Nudge.

'Tracks lead straight to the mesa.'

'Then let's go!' said Ned, starting to lift his reins.

'Hold it! You can read these here tracks from the saddle. Yet, before, we had to scout all over the country, then dismount to find any sign at all.'

Frank's words were cold and flat. The trio all caught his meaning, but it was Logan who said, 'They're layin' for us.'

'Yeah — likely spotted us on the flats, ran for the high ground to set up an ambush . . . You fellers know this neck of the woods better'n I do. Any other way up there?'

Curly didn't hesitate. 'I know a way. Tracked Steve Macklin in there one day when he was tryin' to shake me.'

'Take the lead,' Frank said, and Curly spurred away immediately, the others following.

It was a long, dangerous climb and they had to dismount twice to cover two sections of trail no wider than a couple of feet. The horses were skittish, their fumbling hoofs scattering rocks over the side.

The air was heavy and moist, rain still hanging about in the leaden clouds falling away to the horizon. They swore at the heat and were still cursing when Curly led the way into some brush and thin timber on top of the mesa. Insects stuck to their sweat-beaded flesh.

As Bryant had said earlier, they were going to have to earn their share of that *dinero*.

He was much closer to the truth than he knew.

They were giving the horses a breather, Curly even rubbing down his dun with a handful of leaves, when the first shot cracked. Curly slammed face-first against his startled horse which reared and whinnied and knocked him over the edge with its violent lunge. He screamed all the way down so obviously the bullet hadn't killed him. But there was no way he could walk — or even crawl — away from a fall like that.

The others, all men used to gunfire and reacting accordingly, scattered, dragging rifles free of their saddle-scabbards as they dived for cover. Frank rolled in under a bush, working the lever on his Winchester as he did so. He flopped on to his belly as lead tore through the brush above him, *thru-uuupppped!* into the soft earth so that he had to spit leaves and grit.

Half-a-dozen guns were hammering, raking the brush, meaning to pin them down and to keep them that way: there would be nowhere to go. A trail too steep to use as a getaway behind, blazing guns waiting in front.

If ever there was a true point between a rock and a hard place, this had to be it, thought Bryant, as he worked in closer under his bush. He pushed his rifle ahead and got off five fast, raking shots at a point beneath a cloud of rolling blue-grey gunsmoke upslope.

'Someone else knew about that trail up here!' he heard Ned Nudge say, griping as usual. But he agreed with him.

They'd ridden into a trap.

Then he ducked as fresh bullets tore up the brush and earth around him, lying half on his back as he thumbed in fresh loads. His hat jerked as a bullet clipped the brim and trail dust spattered in front of his face.

Gunfire roared unceasingly: someone up there had spent some time in the army, Frank figured. He kept at least two of his men shooting all the time, not giving the pursuers time to draw proper bead.

It was enough for Frank Bryant. They

were all going to die here on the edge of the damn mesa unless someone did something — and quickly. He slid back, working on knees and elbows in a reverse crawl and suddenly felt his legs waving in mid-air. *Hell almighty!* he hadn't thought he was that close to the edge.

Then Ned grunted an instant after Frank heard a thump like a cleaver cutting into a lump of meat. Ned's body rolled violently to the side and would have crashed into Bryant if he had not used his rifle to stop the man's slide — Ned could have easily taken them both over the edge.

Nudge looked at him with pain-shocked eyes and Frank saw the bullet had taken him high up in the body. He didn't see an exit wound and hoped the lead hadn't gone on down inside and torn up vital organs. Then Ned gritted, 'Bastard! That was . . . Dutch Kernahan . . . got . . . me. Lemme go . . . '

Frank heaved him out of danger of sliding over. As Ned started shooting, wildly, but shooting nonetheless, Bryant eased his lower body over the edge. Rifle in one hand, the other sliding along, finding precarious grips, he dragged himself slowly to the right, legs hanging in space.

It was a tremendous strain but he jammed the rifle butt into the ground so as to take some of his weight. The shooting continued.

He concentrated on working further around the mesa, his boots finding the odd projecting stone to give him enough grip to support his weight. There were low rocks overgrown with brush here and he dragged himself up with a final, grunting heave, flopped and clawed his way in amongst the rocks.

Breathing hard, he held his fire, pulled right up against two small boulders in front of him, screened by a half-dead bush. *He was further round than he had hoped. Not only that, he was on ground slightly higher than the place chosen by McLane and his killers.*

Without hesitation, Frank threw the rifle to his shoulder and started shooting down into the men he could just make out sprawled amongst rocks, ten feet below and about fifty feet distant. His first slug smashed the spine of the man he knew only as 'Irish' or 'Paddy': the body jumped and fell back, stilled on the instant.

The man next to him gave a start and rolled halfway Round, figuring the shot had to come from above somewhere. But he looked too far off to his right and gave Bryant a clear shot. The second bullet took Dutch Kernahan in the head and Carlos let out a yell as he was splashed with blood.

The Mexican reared-up, turning, and Logan, down the slope, picked him off cleanly with a bullet through the neck. By now the others had realized someone was behind them and they started to turn. McLane yelled for them to watch the front as well.

For a few seconds, McLane and his men were caught in a crossfire, rifles and sixguns blazing and tearing the grey day apart with their thunder. The man known as Mannix leapt to his feet in panic and tried to run back to where the horses were. Frank was sure two of his own bullets hit the man, turning him violently, in time to take two or three more from the men down-slope. He jerked and twisted as if someone was yanking on strings and then he fell, crumpling as if his bones had turned to water.

Suddenly the parched brush burst into flame and Frank triggered at the blurred shape of a crouching man running along with handfuls of burning grass, igniting whatever he could. The gun hammer fell on an empty chamber and he dropped the rifle, snatched his sixgun and ran for the man, shooting.

The smoke hid his target. He coughed and wiped a hand across suddenly stinging eyes, hearing Logan yelling to the wounded Ned Nudge to quit shooting or he would hit Frank.

Two more bullets punched air close

to Bryant's head, sending him diving for cover. The man with the burning grass had dropped his fireball, now whipped up his own sixgun in a blur of speed and punched two fast shots. One came close enough to tug violently at a loose fold of Frank's shirt, the bullet just searing his flesh.

He saw it was Carey Budd and hurled himself forward, Colt thrust out ahead, held in a two-handed grip, working hammer-spur and trigger until the gun was empty. Panting, completing one more full roll, he came up on his knees, already thumbing open the loading gate, reaching into his belt loops for fresh shells.

He stopped in mid-action. The Widowmaker was on his knees, one hand pressed against his stomach as blood and intestines fought to get free. There was more blood trickling from a corner of his mouth and his glazing eyes were filled with pain as he glared at Frank. Looking like something from the nether world, Budd brought up his smoking Colt with a mighty effort, steadied it, and thumbed back the hammer.

A rifle whiplashed and Carey Budd jerked sideways, his gun exploding and jumping from his hand as he went down, skidding, sliding to the very edge of the mesa. Still reloading, Bryant walked down and stood over the man who was, amazingly, still alive, his mouth full of blood.

Frank put a boot under one shoulder and heaved and the Widowmaker fell out into space, with one final gurgling scream . . .

Bryant looked for Logan. The outlaw's face was smeared with gunpowder and dirt and a little blood from a bullet burn across his temple.

'Obliged, Logan,' Frank said.

'Weren't me.' Logan told him. He pointed to Ned Nudge, lying on his side now, examining his wound, his smoking rifle beside him.

'Ned?' Frank was surprised.

Nudge scowled. 'Go to hell, Bryant. I

don't owe you . . . nothin' . . . now.'

'Thanks, anyway.' Frank turned to Logan. 'McLane?'

Logan shook his head as he rubbed at his temple, blinking, swaying. 'Got away in the smoke.' Logan fell to his knees as Bryant ran for his horse, hit leather in a flying leap. He wheeled the protesting animal through the veil of smoke that was dissipating now as the flames subsided, having consumed most of the sparse brush up here.

He skidded the mount on to the down trail and hauled rein, not wanting to hit it too fast and risk going over the edge.

He had only gone a few yards when there came the rattle of gunfire from below, the trail hidden by a bend and some of the smoke from the dying fire. Frank slowed, cocked gun in hand as he eased the reluctant horse on. He dismounted before going around the bend but kept a hold of the reins.

There were blurred images of three people and prancing horses. One was a woman! *God almighty! It was Angela McLane!*

The shock froze Frank and a bullet tore his hat off and lifted his hair, causing him to go down to one knee. He kept his grip on the reins and the horse snorted and jerked back, yanking him full-length as the gun fired again. The bullet would have hit him if he hadn't fallen.

He brought up his gun as Angela screamed, and he saw that a desperate-looking McLane had grabbed her around the waist, pulled her in front of him. A puff of wind cleared the smoke. There was a third man down on the trail: Doc Hubbard, clad as usual in his buckskin robe that was now splashed with blood. A rifle lay on the trail near him.

'Drop it, Bryant! Or I'll kill her!' McLane sounded calm enough but his eyes were wild and his gun barrel was rammed hard into the struggling Angela's side.

'Don't struggle, Angela!' Frank

called, afraid her writhing might set the gun off. 'McLane, I'm placing my gun on the ground — OK? I'll do it slow . . . '

'You better!'

Bryant leaned forward, left hand held out in front of him, not taking his eyes off the rancher.

'He — he'll kill her . . . anyway!' hissed the wounded Doc Hubbard.

'Know that, Doc. But I don't have any choice . . . '

Bryant skidded his gun along the ground and for a brief instant, McLane's eyes followed it.

Frank snatched up Doc's rifle lying on the trail, having seen the hammer was already cocked; he twisted as his fist closed around the stock, and fired one-handed.

Angela screamed and collapsed, almost dragging the startled McLane with her. He released her, stared briefly as she hit the dirt and flopped on her face. A twisted smile curled his lips as he said, 'Christ! You killed her yourself!'

His gun lifted. Frank worked the rifle lever faster than he had ever worked one before in his life — three times, hand and metal blurring, the rifle jerking as the shots thundered and punched McLane backwards, mouth open to scream but no life left in him to make a sound.

Except the death-rattle.

Frank knelt beside the girl and she moaned, her teeth biting into her lower lip as she grasped her bleeding leg in the dusty jeans, now wet with her blood. Her eyes reflected the pain she was feeling as she looked at him.

'Sorry — but I had to get you out of the line of fire,' he said.

'You deliberately . . . shot me?'

'It was the only way.' He tore off his neckerchief and wrapped it tightly over her thigh. She winced and a little blood trickled from her lower lip as her teeth sank deep into the flesh. 'Damn you, Frank Bryant!'

Uncomfortable, he stood up, turning towards Doc Hubbard who was lying on his side. The bullet had bounced off a rib and Doc was losing a deal of blood. Frank cut strips from the long buckskin robe and bound them firmly over the wound, Doc gritting his teeth.

'What're you doin' up here anyway?' Bryant asked.

'Angela was worried about you,' Doc told him.

Before Frank could digest that, Logan and Ned Nudge came limping down leading the horses. Logan, still a trifle groggy, held the reins of McLane's claybank and led it back, grinning, pointing to the dusty valise still tied to the cantle.

'Ned and me decided we might's well take it all.'

Ned brought out the sixgun he had been hiding behind his back, thumb awkwardly cocking the hammer.

'You had a deal!' snapped Bryant, but Ned smiled crookedly and shook his head.

'We're makin' a new one, ain't we, Logan?'

The young outlaw leader nodded as he lifted his Colt and said, 'Sorry, folks, but the likes of Ned and me'll never get another chance like this — '

'Not even this one!' Frank said, bringing up the rifle — but the hammer *clicked*! on a fired shell and Ned and Logan merely looked at him until he shrugged and stooped to set down the rifle.

Ned fired and his bullet struck Frank's sixgun that was lying on the trail, skidding it over the edge. He kicked Frank's rifle after it, went to McLane's body and took his sixgun and tossed it over, too.

'Looks like we hold all the aces, Bryant,' he smirked. But his eyes were turning mean and Frank tensed.

'Not all, Ned,' said Doc Hubbard quietly, and a Colt roared, the sound muffled some as it fired through the folds of his buckskin robe.

The bullet took Ned between the eyes and he toppled, rolled and skidded over the edge. Then Doc shot Logan squarely through the heart. The outlaw dropped like a stone.

As Doc clambered awkwardly to his feet, still holding his smoking gun, Bryant and the girl stared at him, stunned.

He shouldered Frank roughly aside and grabbed the reins of McLane's skittish claybank. He fired two shots over the backs of the other restless horses and, whinnying, they plunged down the trail, manes and tails streaming. Doc took Logan's sixgun and put it somewhere under his robe.

'Looks like *I* hold all the aces now.' His pistol came up as Frank moved. 'No, Frank. I told you about my wild days in Montreal and the theft of all that money — what I didn't mention was that I was one of the men McLane stole it from.'

'Funny — I can believe that now.'

Doc smiled thinly. 'About a year ago, after a long search, I finally tracked down Rivelle — McLane. I knew he must still have much of that money but I couldn't get near him with all his bodyguards. I'd travelled once with a religious fanatic who had set up his own sect and lived in the wilds. No one bothered him. So I formed the tribe where I could keep an eye on McLane.'

He paused and frowned slightly. 'Funny thing, I really did get something out of that — a kind of peace I'd never known before.' Then he squared his shoulders. 'I watched and waited, took in Logan and his men, hoping to use them, but they were amateurs. Hopeless — I simply couldn't think of ways of getting my hands on that money. Then, you showed up, Frank, and frightened McLane into running with it. It was like an answer to a prayer, enough to make a man almost believe there is a God.'

'Don't blaspheme, you hypocrite!' snapped Angela. 'I don't care where that money originated, after what Brad put me through, I deserve half!'

Doc nodded. 'And I agree, my dear, but that doesn't mean I'm going to give it to you.' He jerked his gun barrel. 'Lie face down on the ground with your arms stretched over your head. *Now!*'

They obeyed and he climbed awkwardly into the saddle. '*Adios*, brother and sister. I hope we never meet again. You should be able to catch a horse by sundown, but whether or not I feel you will survive . . . Perhaps I'll even live to regret that . . . but for now, farewell.'

He spurred away down-trail, favouring his wounded side.

They got to their feet and Frank sat on a rock and began to roll a cigarette. Angela watched him, unsteady on her feet. She leaned on the rock to take some of the weight off her wounded leg.

'Aren't we going after him?'

'He's got all the guns and we're afoot.'

'But that's *my* money!'

'You're alive, Angela. Settle for that.'

'I'll give you half — half the hundred thousand, if you'll — come with me.' She broke off when she saw his face and sighed. 'Oh, damn you! I've never met a man like you!'

'You won't miss it because you never

really had it, Angela. And you're the best-lookin' woman I've ever met. S'pose we could explore that a bit more . . . ?'

She frowned, unbending. Then suddenly her eyes softened and she smiled.

'Frank Bryant! You're one of a kind!'

'I could use some company,' he grinned wearily.

Their hands reached for each other across the rock and as they embraced for the first time, Angela thought, *One day I'll get him to change his mind — one day*.

THE END

Other titles in the
Linford Western Library:

MIDNIGHT LYNCHING

Terry Murphy

When Ruby Malone's husband is lynched by a sheriff's posse, Wells Fargo investigator Asa Harker goes after the beautiful widow expecting her to lead him to the vast sum of money stolen from his company. But Ruby has gone on the outlaw trail with the handsome, young Ben Whitman. Worse still, Harker finds he must deal with a crooked sheriff. Without help, it looks as if he will not only fail to recover the stolen money but also lose his life into the bargain.

BRAZOS STATION

Clayton Nash

Caleb Brett liked his job as deputy
sheriff and being betrothed to the
sheriff's daughter, Rose. What he
didn't like was the thought of the
sheriff moving in with them once
they were married. But capturing
the infamous outlaw Gil Bannerman
offered a way out because there was
plenty of reward money. Then came
Brett's big mistake — he lost
Bannerman and was framed. Now
everything he treasured was lost.
Did he have a chance in hell of
fighting his way back?

DEAD IS FOR EVER

Amy Sadler

After rescuing Hope Bennett from the clutches of two trailbums, Sam Carver made a serious mistake. He killed one of the outlaws, and reckoned on collecting the bounty on Lew Daggett. But catching Sam off-guard, Daggett made off with the girl, leaving Sam for dead. However, he was only grazed and once he came to, he set out in search of Hope. When he eventually found her, he was forced into a dramatic showdown with his life on the line.

SMOKING STAR

B. J. Holmes

In the one-horse town of Medicine Bluff two men were dead. Sheriff Jack Starr didn't need the badge on his chest to spur him into tracking the killer. He had his own reason for seeking justice, a reason no-one knew. It drove him to take a journey into the past where he was to discover something else that was to add even greater urgency to the situation — to stop Montana's rivers running red with blood.